INVITING TROUBLE

KYLIE GILMORE

Amy,
A best friend's little
sister spells trouble!
Kylie

First Edition: January 2017
Cover design by Kim Killion
Published by: Extra Fancy Books

ISBN-10: 1-942238-26-6
ISBN-13: 978-1-942238-26-3

Because a romance book club would rock...

CHAPTER ONE

10 Years Ago…

Fifteen-year-old Madison Campbell put her hands on her hips and scowled at herself in the mirror as if that would transform her into the beautiful petite kind of girl Parker Shaw was into. She had to make this beauty thing work because Park, the guy she'd worshipped for as long as she could remember, was about to leave town with her virginity.

He just didn't know it yet.

She lifted her shoulder-length dark brown hair, trying to figure out how to make it stay up in a twist like she'd seen Miss Popular, Shannon, do. She grabbed a ponytail holder, wrapped it around the mass of hair, and let go. It flopped to the side. "Donkey balls," she muttered, yanking the hair band out and tossing it across the counter.

How did girls do this? She had no one to ask. Her own mom had split when Mad was only one. She was the only girl, no, the only *woman*, in the house with five older brothers and her dad. All of her friends were guys too. Every time she tried to hang with girls, she felt like she'd accidentally put on the Spanish channel. It all sounded good, but she had no idea what they were talking about. There were good crushes and bad crushes, which seemed like pretty much the same thing to her. And stuff that sounded like a question but wasn't. So what if she didn't speak fluent girl? She had no problem talking to guys, even an insanely hot guy like Park. She just had to show him she wasn't that mouthy twerp he'd grown up with.

She shoved her hands in her hair and tried to fluff it up for that natural wavy look she'd seen on TV. Now it looked kind of frizzy. She turned on the faucet and splashed water all over her head, smoothing it down again. Forget the hair. She grabbed the pink lipstick she'd filched from Shannon's purse in the locker room during gym and puckered up. Mad wasn't afraid of sex. She knew everything already, what went where, the condom part, the noises girls made. She had her tomcat brothers to thank for that, sneaking girls home when their dad was at work. She swiped the lipstick across her top lip and then kept going full circle to the bottom lip and back to the top. She carefully capped the lipstick, planning on returning it to Shannon on Monday at school when she wasn't looking.

She smiled in the mirror and then stopped. She looked like a clown. It was too bright, made for Shannon's blonde fairer looks, and sort of smeared. She grabbed a tissue and scrubbed it off. This was stupid. She knew what guys liked—big tits.

She looked down at herself. B cup. She grabbed her boobs with both hands and squeezed them together, trying to make some cleavage. Nothing impressive. She yanked her favorite black concert shirt down and lifted her boobs at the same time. Better. She grabbed the top of the shirt with both hands, a favorite hand-me-down from her brother, Ty, hesitated for a split second and then ripped it into a V-neck. Still no cleavage. She ripped the shirt a little lower. She leaned forward and moved her shoulders side to side. There. Now you could definitely tell she had boobs.

What else? She reached for Shannon's blue eye shadow, swabbed a bunch on the little wand and swiped it across her lids. She opened her dark brown eyes to check out the dramatic results. Suckage. She'd clearly lifted makeup from the wrong girl. No point in trying the blue eyeliner. She should've filched something from Shannon's dark-haired friend Michelle. She blew out a breath. She'd just have to use her body.

She turned sideways in the mirror, throwing her shoulders back, and then turned and looked at her ass. Kind of flat. She looked nothing like the curvy centerfolds in those magazines her brothers hid under their mattresses. She was five foot four with a thin, boyish, athletic bod. Not as petite as Park's last curvy little girlfriend. She put her hands on her waist. She did have a narrow waist. Maybe if she hiked up the shirt, the narrow waist would give the appearance of more curve in the hip.

She tied the shirt in two knots just above her hip bones, showing off her belly button. She briefly considered attempting a safety-pin piercing to draw attention to her belly button, which was a nice innie, but feared it would look too red. She'd pierced her own ear and, man, that had been red for a whole day.

Someone pounded on the door. "Hurry up! I gotta take a whiz!" a male voice barked.

"Use the other bathroom!" she hollered back.

He jiggled the knob. She'd locked it, of course. *Bam. Bam. Bam.* Had to be Ty. He was the most physical of her brothers. He'd kick the door open if she didn't hurry. She shoved the evidence—lipstick, eye gunk—into her jeans pockets.

"Come on, Mad. It's an emergency. Logan is in the other bathroom."

"He's probably just whacking off," she said,

pulling her hair forward over her shoulders, hoping to draw attention to her boobs.

Boom. The door shook. He must've kicked it.

She rolled her eyes and gave herself one last long look. Would Park want this? She didn't know what else she could do to improve the picture. She sniffed her pits. Smelled okay. She should've swiped some perfume too.

Boom. The door rattled. "What the hell are you doing in there?" Ty boomed.

She opened the medicine cabinet, hoping there might be something that smelled good, but it was just her brothers' crap. Most of them still lived at home, except identical twins Jake and Josh, who were in the Army.

"Mad!"

She sighed, turned, and yanked open the door.

"Get out of the way," Ty said, not bothering to give her the chance. He grabbed her by the waist and lifted her into the hallway. Like all her brothers, he was tall, nearly six foot, brown hair, brown eyes, and bulging with muscles. At twenty-one, he worked at the gym, teaching other people how to get strong. The door slammed behind him.

She headed to the small room she shared with her older brother by three years, Logan. She got the top bunk. Their house only had three bedrooms. Her dad hogged one of them all to himself, though he took the smallest bedroom. The master bedroom had two sets of bunk beds for the four oldest boys. Park had the living room sofa. Her dad had rescued him from a bad home when he was ten and she was seven, and he'd been living with them ever since. She couldn't imagine how she would've survived her brothers without Park. He'd always looked out for her. Who always picked her to be on their team when no one wanted her? Park. Who gave her their ice cream when her brothers devoured the tub before she got a single drop? Park. Who shut her brothers up when her feelings got hurt? The guy soon to take her virginity—Park.

And tomorrow he left for the Air Force for six long years. Her throat got tight. *Don't cry*, she told herself. *You can cry all you want once he's gone.*

She squeezed her eyes shut and took a deep breath. She had an hour before the going-away party. Her dad had taken Park out to dinner, just the two of them. She opened the closet, kicked some of Logan's cleats out of the way and tried to decide between sneakers and her black combat boots. Which one said petite pretty girl? Sneakers. Definitely. They were white and mostly clean. She grabbed them, grabbed a handful of tissues and sat on the floor to clean them up.

She spat into the tissue and rubbed at a scuff on the toe, thinking of Park again. Would he see her with new eyes tonight? Would he notice she was different? All grown up? She'd shot up to her full height at twelve, but now she had the body to go with it. He *had* to notice. And if he didn't, she'd just wrap her arms around his neck and kiss him. Actions always spoke louder than words. She'd never kissed a guy, but she'd spied on her brothers before. It couldn't be that hard if they'd managed it.

She lifted the back of her hand to practice. Easy. She opened her mouth and added some tongue action.

"What're you doing?" Ty asked from the doorway.

She jolted and dropped her hand, her cheeks burning. "Ever hear of knocking?"

Ty leaned against the doorframe in a sleeveless shirt and shorts, crossing his arms like he always did to show off his bulging biceps. "Door was open." He smirked. "Were you French-kissing your hand?"

She hurled her sneaker at him.

He ducked and grinned. "Who you gonna kiss, huh?"

"I wasn't kissing my hand. I was spitting. Cleaning my sneaks." She stood and shoved one foot into a mostly clean sneak, retrieved the other one near Ty, and slipped it on.

"Did you rip my favorite shirt?" Ty asked. "Mad!"

She lifted her chin. "It hasn't fit you in five years. It's mine and I can do what I want with it. This is the style."

He pointed at her chest. "I can see your…your…cover up!"

She set her teeth. "No."

He stared at the two knots she'd made at the bottom of the shirt, stared at her belly button, then went to the dresser, yanked open a drawer, and grabbed another hand-me-down, a faded Eastman High track shirt, and tossed it at her. "Put that on."

"No." She stepped around the shirt and headed out.

"Dad's not gonna let you out of the house like that," Ty called.

"I'm not going out," she threw over her shoulder, heading for the stairs. She halted on the top step when the front door opened and the man of her dreams stepped inside.

Her heart thumped its love beat—*Park*-er, *Park*-er, *Park*-er. *Be cool!* Park's dark brown hair was in a buzz cut, ready for basic training, his wide shoulders straining the fabric of a white T-shirt with faded jeans that molded to his body. He was eighteen, enlisted to serve his country, a full-fledged man. He looked up, his gorgeous hazel eyes meeting hers, and she slowly descended the stairs in what she hoped was a sexy and alluring way.

"Hey, little bit," Park said with a smile. "We got

an ice cream cake."

Little bit. Her heart sank. Little bit, mini, shortstack. She was *always* the little twerp. Did he even notice she was all woman?

Her dad—a tall fit man with short brown hair, brown eyes, and what she called laugh lines around his eyes and mouth, and he called worry lines on account of all his kids—stepped inside with the cake. He gave her a quick hello and headed to the kitchen.

She rushed down the rest of the stairs, eager for Park to get a closer look at her boobs. Seriously, if even Ty noticed her low-cut shirt, Park had to. Park always noticed her, always looked out for her and included her when her brothers told her to get lost.

"We should set up the volleyball net in the backyard," Park told her, looking around. "Where is everyone?"

She stopped directly in front of him, the tips of their sneakers nearly touching. "I'm here."

He put a large hand on top of her head. "Yeah. Where's everyone else?"

She silently seethed, but didn't push his hand away. At least he was touching her.

"Mad, we've got to get you some new clothes," her dad said, returning from the kitchen. "That shirt's falling apart. Go change and then run the vacuum while I get stuff ready."

Park dropped his hand and his gaze locked on her chest. She threw her shoulders back to make the view more impressive. He met her eyes again. "Ty here?"

"Upstairs," she said and stomped upstairs to change.

Ty brushed past her and headed downstairs, calling to Park, "Hey, you're back! I got beer."

Mad's ears perked up. Maybe if Park had a beer or two, he might be easier to convince. She knew her dad wouldn't mind if Park drank. After Park had enlisted, he and her dad had a beer together, toasting to Park's future. She went to the larger bedroom where Park kept his stuff, grabbed his dark blue plaid flannel shirt, and pulled it on. Now she was covered and he'd notice she was wearing his shirt. She made it to the hallway when she realized her mistake. It was July and, even in the air-conditioning, she was sweating. She quickly changed out of jeans and into some shorts. The flannel shirt fell a little low, over her hips, just a bit of shorts peeking out. Cool.

She did the stupid vacuuming, got even sweatier, and had to put her hair up in a high ponytail. So much for sexy style. By the time the house was filled with her brothers and their friends, her sleeves were rolled up and all the buttons of Park's flannel shirt undone. Her dad didn't notice her boobs were back on display. He was too busy holding court in his favorite recliner, reminiscing about his old Army days. She sat on the arm of the sofa; Park sat on the far end away from her. In between were her brothers Ty and Alex. Logan sat on the floor with their blood brothers—like family, these guys were—Zach, Ethan, Ben, and Marcus. Her dad, a cop, was active in the Police Athletic League and mentored a lot of kids who needed a stable father figure in their lives.

She pretended to listen while she mentally rehearsed what she'd say to Park later, once everyone was gone or asleep. She'd sneak downstairs to where he slept on the sofa and she'd say…what? She bit her lip and looked over at him. He met her eyes and winked.

She flushed and quickly looked away. Did he know what she was thinking? That would make it so much easier.

Her dad finally wound down and Ty spoke up. "Park's not the only one heading out. I'm going to LA next month."

"What? Why?" Everyone spoke at once.

Ty grinned. Only Park didn't seem surprised. The two were close. "I'm going to be a stuntman."

"How you gonna do that?" Alex asked. He was in community college and still trying to figure out what to do with his life.

"I met a guy at the gym who used to do it," Ty said. "He's gonna set me up with some people he knows."

"You make sure you get the right training," their dad said. "Don't be reckless and get yourself killed."

"Come on," Ty said, pointing at himself with both hands. "With this bod? You know I take care of the goods." He flexed his guns.

Everyone laughed except Mad, who just sat there, eyes hot. One by one, the guys were leaving. First Jake and Josh had left for the Army, then Ethan to the police academy, Park to the Air Force, and now Ty. Pretty soon she'd be like an only child. Everything was changing and she hated it. She got up and went to the kitchen, needing a minute to herself. How could everyone be so happy about their whole family falling apart?

She dug around in the fridge, grabbed one of Ty's beers, and looked for the bottle opener. She found it in the junk drawer. She'd just popped the top when it was snatched out of her hands.

"Thanks, mini," Park said, tossing the drink back.

She scowled.

He fixed her with a hard look. "You're too young to drink."

"No one cares," she said. "It's a party."

"*I* care."

She swallowed over the lump in her throat. No one would ever care about her the way Park did. He noticed her. He made her feel special.

Park leaned against the counter and set the beer out of her reach. "You upset about Ty leaving?"

"Everyone's leaving," she muttered.

"Everyone's grown up," he said. "It's time."

She was quiet, glad he'd included her in that grown-up bit, glad to have him all to herself. She hopped up on the counter next to him, swinging her legs. "I'll probably leave soon too."

He inclined his head. "You'll get there. You keep getting As, you could go to college."

"By the time you get back, I could almost be done college."

He pulled out his cell. "We'll keep in touch. Email, text, whatever." He held up his cell. "Say cheese."

"Cheese," she said and smiled with all the love in her heart.

He looked at the picture, grunted, and shoved the cell in his pocket.

She studied his profile, the surge of love overwhelming in its intensity. "Park, I—"

"Hey!" Ty boomed, coming into the kitchen. "Time for volleyball. Move it on out." He snagged a beer for himself and headed out the back door. The guys followed close behind, already divvying up the teams. Her dad went with them.

She started to follow when Park grabbed her by the back of the collar.

"You're gonna sweat like a pig in this," he said. "What're you wearing my shirt for anyway?"

She peeled off the flannel shirt and handed it to him. Then she pulled the V in her concert shirt down lower. "My shirt ripped. See?"

He looked and then his eyes snapped to hers. "Did *you* rip it?"

She lifted her chin. "Yeah. It's the style."

"Who's the guy?"

"No guy, moron," she said and stalked out the door before he could see her blush.

He caught up with her, grabbed her collar in the back and pulled, this time to cover her up. The shirt shifted so the gap hung loose in back. Before she could say some smartass remark, he jogged past her and over to the other side of the net.

Mad bided her time at the party, playing volleyball, shooting hoops, sneaking sips of her brothers' beer, until it was late and her dad wanted to make a toast before he shut down the party. He'd be driving Park early the next morning to the airport where he'd catch a flight to basic training in Texas.

Her dad raised his beer. "To Park, we're proud of you and glad to call you family."

Park raised his bottle of beer and took them all in.

"I'm grateful to have you as my family." His voice was gruff with emotion, which made her eyes hot and her throat tight.

"Hear, hear," Ty said and they all drank.

Finally the party broke up and the guys scattered. Some to their beds, some to their apartments. She went to her room, lying in bed for a long time, until the house got quiet and she was sure Logan was sleeping. Then she snuck downstairs, wearing only the long T-shirt she slept in. She'd stashed a condom in the back of the coffee table drawer for just this moment, stolen from Logan's sock drawer. It was dark, but she had plenty of practice sneaking around.

She made her way to the sofa, where Park was sprawled under a blue comforter. "Park," she whispered.

No response.

She jabbed him in the arm. "Park."

Still nothing. She sat on the sofa next to him and jabbed him in the ribs. "Park, it's Mad. Wake up."

He groaned and shifted. She jabbed him again. His eyes opened. "What?"

She leaned close, so close their lips nearly touched. "I'm going to miss you," she said softly.

He closed his eyes. "Oh, man, the room's spinning. I drank too much."

She leaned back. "How much did you drink?"

He waved his hand around. "I dunno. Eight beers. Me and Ty had one last party. So-oo wasted."

She hadn't noticed him drinking a lot. That wasn't like Park. In fact, she could count on one hand the number of times he'd had too much to drink. Maybe twice, both times with Ty.

She turned on the lamp on the end table and peered at him. He squinted. She got close and stared into his eyes. "Your eyes don't look drunk."

"I'm feeling it, believe me." He turned off the light and flopped back down on his side. "Go to bed, mini."

She got brave and stroked a hand through his hair, the rough short ends tickling her palm. "Your hair feels different." He used to have shaggy soft hair. She liked to mess it up sometimes. He didn't push her away, so she let her fingers trail to the warm skin of his neck. "I'm not mini anymore," she told him. "I'm all grown up."

He rolled to his back and threw an arm over his eyes. "Let me sleep this off," he said, his words slurring. "Seriously. Wa-a-ay too much to drink."

Maybe he was drunk. She sat there for a few minutes, soaking in the heat of him, the scent of fresh soap and sexy man. His breathing deepened into sleep. She wanted to lie next to him, just to sleep since he was wasted, but he unexpectedly shifted, bumping her off the sofa. She stood and looked down at him, trying to memorize his features in the dim light from the streetlights through the front window. The thick lashes resting on his cheeks, the high cheekbones, the square jaw. He was the most beautiful man she'd ever seen.

She knelt next to the sofa, leaned over and brushed her lips across his, stealing a kiss. A tingle went through her. She did it again, fitting her lips more firmly against his, and gasped when he was suddenly kissing her back. His lips moved expertly over hers and heat surged through her body. His tongue touched the seam of her lips, she opened for him, and his tongue thrust inside. She couldn't help the moan that escaped as her body urged her to get closer.

And then it was over. He groaned and rolled to his side, giving her his back.

"Park," she whispered, "I want you to be my first."

He was quiet.

She stood and leaned over him. He seemed to be asleep. Maybe all that beer made him extra sleepy. She'd only ever had one beer and it had made her feel stupid-happy and then tired. She watched him for long minutes and finally stroked his hair one last time. "Come back in one piece, okay?"

Her eyes stung with tears and she rushed upstairs. Sleep was impossible. She tossed and turned all night and got out of bed the moment she heard movement downstairs. She wouldn't miss saying goodbye. She quickly dressed, brushed her teeth and hair, and hurried downstairs. Park was neatly folding his blanket and tucking it away in the coat closet. It was early and everyone was still sleeping.

"Is Dad up?" she asked.

"Yeah. He went to get bagels for everyone." He shoved a hand through his hair. "Man, I've got a killer hangover. I barely remember the party."

She studied him, unsure if he was being serious or not. Did he really not remember *anything*? "How drunk were you?"

He shook his head. "I don't even know how I got to the sofa. One minute I'm chugging beer with Ty, next minute I'm out cold."

She swallowed hard. He really didn't remember. He hadn't meant to kiss her back. It was a reflex. Probably any guy would do that if someone kissed them. Her first kiss was a joke. What if she'd slept with him and he didn't remember it? That would've been horrible.

"Yeah, you were totally wasted," she said.

The front door opened and her dad appeared with a bag of bagels and a to-go coffee. "Park and I gotta run." He jerked his chin at Park. "Five minutes," he said before heading to the kitchen.

Park went upstairs for a few minutes and returned with a duffel bag. "The guys are sleeping. I said bye to them last night."

Mad waited. Her last chance for a goodbye. Her last chance with the love of her life.

Her dad took the duffel bag and headed to the car.

Park looked at her for a long moment, his hazel eyes direct. "Study hard, okay? Keep your grades up."

Her lower lip wobbled. "You're not my dad."

He wrapped her in a big bear hug and kissed the top of her head. Her eyes welled. He pulled back and ruffled her hair. "Bye, little bit."

He left, the door shutting quietly behind him.

CHAPTER TWO

Present day…

"What do you think about a sex-toy party?" Mad asked casually, then waited for the fireworks. Her friends from the Happy Endings Book Club, a romance book club that Mad had somehow gotten roped into two years ago, were at her house, helping her decorate for Park's homecoming party.

Hailey Adams, leader of their book club and Clover Park's one and only wedding planner, slammed her hands on her hips and glared. "How did we get from what do you think about a paranormal romance selection to sex toys?"

Mad jerked her chin. "I thought we were playing the *what do you think about* game."

Charlotte Vega, a personal trainer with brassy confidence, bumped Mad with her hip. "You're as bad as your brother." She meant her older brother Josh, who razzed Hailey all the time because Hailey was just that much fun to rile up.

Hailey tossed a pack of balloons at Mad. "Use your hot air for a good cause."

Mad caught them and looked around the living room of the house she'd grown up in, trying to decide where to put balloons. The other women—Hailey, Charlotte, Lauren, Carrie, and Ally—were hanging red, white, and blue streamers around the edges of the room, the windows, and the front door. Park was coming home for good after ten years away in the Air Force. He'd only visited a few times over the years because he'd volunteered for a lot of year-long deployments to classified locations that paid extra for the high risk. Her worry over him was never ending. Every time she saw him, her heart ached something fierce at the way he kept his distance. She told herself it was better that way, easier to say goodbye, but deep down she feared he knew how much she cared about him and just didn't feel the same way. It was embarrassing to admit, but he'd always been the gold standard for her and no man had ever measured up. Now that he was coming home for good, she was determined to breach that distance, to put up or shut up once and for all so she could freaking move on if that was what she had to do.

She still thought all the decorations were too much. Just give a guy a brewski and some cake. Done deal.

Hailey shot her a sweet smile and gestured for her to get moving with the balloons. Mad still didn't know how she ended up with Hailey for a friend. The woman was a former beauty queen with long strawberry blonde hair, pale blue eyes, and a perfect curvy body always tastefully displayed in designer dresses. The kind of girl that would've been homecoming queen and looked down at Mad with her skinny, boyish athletic body in hand-me-down shirts, ripped jeans, and black combat boots. She glared at the balloons, pissed at how emotional she'd been all day today. The decorations were beside the point. The women, the first women friends she'd ever had, were here for moral support. That was all Hailey's doing, who somehow read between the lines with all Mad couldn't express.

"Guys," Mad croaked.

The women looked over at her. No words could get through the emotion clogging her throat. She'd hardly slept last night she was so nervous about seeing Park and finally letting him know just how much she felt for him. It meant so damn much that her friends were here for her.

"We should start the party early with some beer," Mad finally said, completely inadequately. She never did get the hang of girl talk. All she knew was the gruff bluster and joking around she was raised with. She tossed the balloons on the coffee table and headed for the kitchen.

Hailey intercepted her and gave her a warm hug. Mad let her. They were the same size, five foot four, so Mad had to blow Hailey's long hair out of her face. The woman was her best friend, though Mad could never find the words to say so.

Hailey pulled back, her pale blue eyes bright. "I know you're nervous, but you'll do great. You've got this. Hanging with the guys is your thing!"

Mad swallowed hard and gave a quick nod before heading to the kitchen. Hanging with the guys was *not* the same thing as being with Park. Especially now that she'd decided to put it all on the line. She just couldn't live with herself if she didn't try to see what might be there between them. No man had ever gotten close to her heart the way Park did. It was like her heart closed when Park left and only now when it was possible for something between them did it creak open again. Painful fact. Hell, she was strong and fierce and unafraid to face anything or anyone.

So why was she trembling at the thought?

She opened the refrigerator door and stared in shock at the bottle of champagne chilling there. "Hailey?" she called.

"It's for the party!" Hailey caroled back. "In honor

of Park's service to our country."

Mad shoved a hand in her dyed red hair, which was at that awkward growing-out stage after being short for so long. Hailey didn't even know Park. This was so damn thoughtful. *She* should've thought of doing something special like this. She didn't know how to do this guy thing with someone she actually cared about. Her boyfriends were temporary whenever she had the itch for sex, which wasn't that often.

She grabbed a six-pack of lite beer, something her brothers would turn their nose up at, which was the only reason they were still untouched. She snagged the bottle opener and brought them out to the living room. "Six beers for six women. Works out perfectly." She set them on the coffee table and started popping the tops.

Hailey took a sip and wrinkled her nose. "Next time I'll bring wine. So what're you wearing tonight?" She took in Mad's usual outfit—T-shirt, baggy cargo shorts, and black work boots.

Mad glanced down at herself. Okay, so she'd never gotten the hang of women's fashion, and she liked being comfortable, but everything was clean and this was her favorite T-shirt. It read Try Me. She liked it because of the double meaning. Try Me could be a challenge to a fight or seduction as in *you want some of this?* She enjoyed a good fight most of all, especially in the dojo with a well-matched opponent. She was a fourth-degree black belt and skilled with weapons.

"I'm not wearing a dress," Mad said, cutting off Hailey's go-to wardrobe. Hailey was her size but with bigger boobs and frequently offered to lend her an outfit for special occasions. If forced to wear something for a formal occasion, Mad had a black pants suit.

The women studied her and then exchanged looks with each other. Mad squirmed, knowing she wasn't passing the girl test, yet not confident she could pull off the dress thing. She always felt so stiff and uncomfortable in dresses. She flopped on the sofa and propped her feet up on the coffee table.

Charlotte joined her on the sofa, pulling her long brown hair with auburn highlights over one shoulder and twirling it around her hand. "So how hot is he, like panty melting?"

Heat crept up Mad's neck. She jerked her chin and took a long swallow of cold beer.

"Is he nice?" sweet Lauren asked. She was an elementary school teacher.

Mad snorted. "Of course he's nice. He's my blood brother, isn't he?" Blood brother was what they called their honorary brothers, the guys her dad mentored as kids in the Police Athletic League. All of them had become like family.

"Tall, dark, and broody?" Charlotte asked.

Mad picked at the label on the beer bottle, unwilling to admit that was how she remembered Park best. Dark hair, intense hazel eyes that were mostly brown with some lighter green and gold, definitely broody, but also sweet. He'd become more serious after the Air Force, or maybe that was just how it seemed those few times she'd seen him because he'd been so distant.

Hailey sat on Mad's other side. "He's the only guy you ever blush over."

She felt her cheeks heat. "I do not blush. You're delusional."

Carrie, Ally, and Lauren sat cross-legged on the floor around the coffee table and the women all looked to her, waiting for details. She knew what that meant—girl talk. The sharing had begun around books, but now included times like this, just hanging out. Mad liked listening to the talk, but still found it difficult to talk about herself. She was more used to hanging with guys, who were not big into "sharing and caring," as Hailey called it.

Hailey put a hand on Mad's arm. "It doesn't leave this room. You can tell us anything."

She tensed. It was just them, she told herself. Probably another hour before Ty got here with Park. Her dad was upstairs in the shower. The guys wouldn't be here for a few more hours for the party.

"Spill, girl," Charlotte said, elbowing her.

Mad took a deep breath, on the verge of confessing everything because it was eating her up inside. But the words died in her throat when the front door swung open. They never bothered to lock it until everyone was in for the night. She caught a glimpse of a tall man with dark short-cropped hair and leapt off the sofa, banging into the coffee table and spilling her beer in the process. The women rescued their own drinks before they spilled. Her heart raced, her mind a whirl before she realized it was just Alex, her older brother by four years.

"Hello, ladies," Alex said warmly in his smooth voice.

The women sighed as one, except Mad, who rolled her eyes and headed to the kitchen for paper towels. She hated that she was so jittery.

"Dad home?" Alex called.

"Upstairs," she hollered back.

She heard the front door open and close. She'd just returned to the living room when the front door opened again. The women let out a collective, "Awww."

Alex held his sleeping daughter, twenty-month-old Vivian, and went upstairs where her dad kept a crib for her. Alex was a single dad from the very beginning.

His fiancée, Tammy, died during the C-section. It hadn't been easy for Alex to balance work and parenting, but her dad was retired from a long career as a cop and able to help out.

"She looks like an angel," Lauren said. "Those sweet curls and chubby cheeks."

"Only when she's sleeping," Mad replied. Her niece had a bit of the hell-on-wheels Campbell genes.

Alex left, saying he'd be back in an hour. Her dad would look after Viv if she woke.

Hailey went right back to where they'd left off. "Tell us about Park."

Her mind immediately flashed to his going-away party, her last best memory of him, the last time she'd felt close to him. He'd been so drunk, he didn't even remember it. She should focus on that fact, not the fact that she'd completely screwed up the transformation from mouthy twerp to sexy woman. Not the fact that he didn't remember the first kiss of her entire life. And definitely not the fact that she'd offered him her virginity. Too late now! Adrenaline shot through her. She needed a run or a sparring match. Something. Unfortunately it was December, the sidewalks were too icy for a run, and none of these women could match her in sparring. She needed Ty, also a black belt.

She leapt to her feet. "I'll get the chips."

She dashed into the kitchen, threw several controlled punches, and then took a few deep breaths, finding her calm center again, something karate had taught her. She snagged a bag of potato chips, returned to the living room and tossed them on the coffee table. She flopped back on the sofa.

"How long's it been since you've seen him?" Ally asked eagerly. Her blonde hair, ending just past her jaw, bounced a little in her excitement.

Mad fidgeted on the sofa, clenching and unclenching her fists. "Two years. He's been home a few times but we never spent much time together." Not by her choice. It felt more like ten years since they'd really connected. Park had signed on for four more years after his first six were up. Then, once he was out, he'd taken a five-month assignment for a government contractor near the Air Force base, working on a new flight simulator. Now he was finally returning home. He was twenty-eight; she'd turned twenty-six last week. They were like two completely different people than they were back then. Maybe this was all in her head. Maybe there was nothing there anymore.

"Do you have a picture?" Hailey asked.

She pulled her cell out and scrolled through to the picture he'd sent of him in uniform at the ceremony where he was promoted to tech sergeant. She was so damn proud of him. He looked different in the formal uniform, so clean cut, serious, and proud. Not the badass edgy guy with a soft spot for her that she remembered. God, she'd worshipped him as a kid. As a teen too. The women passed around the picture.

"Total hottie," Charlotte proclaimed. The women agreed.

The front door swung open again and her heart galloped madly. But it was just Josh, her oldest brother at thirty-three, well, second oldest technically by two minutes to his identical twin, Jake. Josh had gotten her a job as a part-time bartender at Garner's Sports Bar & Grill, where he worked when she'd moved back home to start college two years ago. He was carrying trays of covered food, most likely from Garner's.

"Hello, Happy Endings ladies," he said with a charming smile that took all of them in, pointedly avoiding Hailey, before heading for the kitchen.

"Sluts!" Mad called after him.

Josh barked out a laugh, and she snickered. Hailey shot her a dark look. It was a callback to the name Mad had suggested for their book club, Super Lovers of Underrated Terrific Stories (SLUTS), just to razz Hailey. Happy Endings Book Club was suggested by another member and it stuck. Pretty tame.

"We should go," Hailey said, standing and gesturing to the rest of them.

"You're leaving already?" Mad croaked.

"You're all set," Hailey said. "Decorations, food. And you said yourself it was family only for the party."

They couldn't leave her yet. She needed her bitches to get through this. At least until Park arrived.

"Just hang out a bit," Mad said.

Hailey shook her head and got her white wool coat from the front closet. She was probably eager to leave because of the feud she and Josh had going on that started with Josh as a paid escort for Hailey's wedding planning business (a truly twisted story) and escalated to epic proportions when Josh had pulled a switcheroo, taking Hailey out to dinner, pretending to be his wealthy twin. Hailey had promised eternal vengeance once she realized she'd been played. Most recently in the feud, Hailey had whispered to some ladies flirting with Josh at Garner's that he had an affliction that left him impotent and he'd had no luck getting a date since. The best part was, he had no idea why. But that shouldn't mean they deserted *her*.

The women stood and gathered their beer bottles; most of them hadn't even finished.

"But you have to finish your beer," Mad said desperately.

Charlotte finished hers in one long swallow while the rest of them watched in awe. She daintily wiped her mouth with her fingertips and smiled. Charlotte was the kind of ballsy girl Mad would've raised hell with in high school. Except Charlotte was five years older and grew up in New Jersey. Whatever. She knew her now and respected her bold confidence and athleticism as a personal trainer.

"Impressive," Mad told Charlotte.

Charlotte slipped on her black down jacket and pulled her long brown hair out of the collar. "Thanks."

Hailey hugged Mad. "Good luck tonight."

"Where are you going?" Mad asked.

Hailey turned to the group. "Happy hour at Garner's?"

"I'll go with you," Mad said.

"That might actually be a good idea," Hailey said. "That way when you return, you can make a grand entrance at the party. Maybe we can stop at my place after drinks. We can do your hair and makeup, and ooh, you can wear one of my dresses, and then it'll be like ta-dah!"

Mad froze at the idea of all that girly fussing over her and the uncomfortable idea of wearing a dress.

"Let's roll," Charlotte said, heading out the door.

The women followed close behind.

"Just drinks," Mad barked and went with them.

At the bar, Mad bought the first round and had a couple shots of tequila herself. Feeling considerably more relaxed, she allowed Charlotte, the most practical effortlessly gorgeous woman she'd ever met, to go with her to the ladies' room and fix her face. She wouldn't fuss too much like Hailey.

"Our coloring is different," Charlotte said, digging through her huge faux leather purse. "But our eyes are similar." Charlotte's skin was a golden tan compared to Mad's fair skin, but they both had brown eyes. "Let's try my eyeliner. Look up."

Mad did, flashing back to that first time she'd attempted makeup for Park and how utterly stupid it had turned out. "I don't usually wear makeup."

"No shit," Charlotte said.

Mad laughed.

Charlotte pulled the liner pencil away. "Don't move or I'll poke your eye out."

Mad got serious, hoping she didn't look like an idiot when this was all done.

Charlotte finished up. "Nice."

Mad turned to the mirror—the brown liner actually made her eyes look dark and sexy. "So you only put it underneath?"

"For your eye shape, yes."

"Oh." She felt stupid that she still didn't know the first thing about makeup. She stared at herself some more, wondering if Park would even notice. If he'd still be cool and distant, still put her in the mouthy-little-twerp slot. She wasn't the mouthy fifteen-year-old she'd been back then, now she was a mouthy twenty-six-year-old. *Fuck my life.*

Charlotte piped up. "You must be freaking out. You look like a deer caught in the headlights."

"Thanks."

Charlotte dug through her purse again. "Was he your first boyfriend? The one that got away? What was he to you?"

The fact that she wasn't looking directly at Mad made it easier to confess. "He was everything. And then he left."

Charlotte opened a deep red lipstick. "Yeah. They do that. Keep your lips together, relaxed." She applied some color to Mad's lips. "What do you think?"

Mad looked in the mirror. "Weird."

Charlotte handed her a paper towel. "Blot it. Like this." She demonstrated with her lips, not quite touching the towel.

Mad copied.

Charlotte tucked the lipstick away and gave Mad a quick once-over. "You look good, girl. You sure you want to go with the cargo shorts and boots?"

"I'm not wearing a dress."

"You got skinny jeans?"

"Yeah."

"Put them on. These shorts make you look huge and I know you're totally fit."

"Whatever," Mad muttered, heading for the door.

Charlotte followed behind. "You're welcome."

Mad turned outside of the bathroom in the hallway. "I'm sorry. Thank you. I'm just worked up. I want to play it cool, but I'm more likely to blurt something stupid."

"Just be yourself."

"Yeah, that'll work," Mad said under her breath. She could do hanging with the guys, she could do insults, she could do hip checks and high fives. What she couldn't do was flirt. When she wanted a guy, she baldly stated it, usually after a game of basketball, softball, or a really good sparring match at the dojo. Parker Shaw was way beyond want. At least he had been. Hell, maybe once she managed to get close to him again, she wouldn't even be attracted to the clean-cut straitlaced military man he'd turned into. Maybe she was freaking out for nothing.

Charlotte nudged her shoulder. "I have complete faith in you."

Mad's throat got tight. They returned to the bar and the women fussed over her makeup. "Shut up, bitches. I'm still the same." Awkward, nervous, and in over her head.

"Well, you're a very pretty bitch now," Hailey said.

Mad's cheeks burned and she quickly took her seat at the bar. Next thing she knew Charlotte had ordered the next round and, after her third tequila, Mad blurted, "I'm not a virgin."

No one was surprised.

"You are twenty-six," Hailey pointed out. The book club had treated her to dinner for her birthday last week. She still couldn't get over how damn nice women friends were to each other. Guys never picked up the tab for dinner.

"I didn't wait for Park and now it's too late," Mad confessed, getting to the heart of the matter.

"Honey, no one waits ten years," Charlotte said in a sympathetic tone.

"Fuck it," Mad said, pounding her fist on the bar.

By the time Hailey dropped her off back home, well into the appointed party time for a grand entrance, Mad was flying high with the women's words of encouragement and a healthy dose of alcohol-fueled confidence. All she needed now was to change into jeans for that hot girl look Charlotte recommended.

"Look out, Park, here I come," she muttered under her breath, making her way unsteadily to the front door for her big *ta-dah* entrance.

CHAPTER THREE

Parker Shaw settled in on the comfortable old brown sofa, his former bunk, with a beer and took in his adopted family, the Campbells, gathered around him. "Damn, it's good to be home."

"It's good to have you home," Joe Campbell said, clapping a hand on Park's shoulder. The older man was as close to a dad as Park ever had. "I'll get the food. Josh, give me a hand."

"We missed your ugly face," Josh said, palming Park's face and giving it a shove.

"Yeah, yeah," Park said.

They headed to the kitchen. It was just him, Ty, Alex, and Alex's toddler daughter, Vivian, who kept climbing the stairs and sliding down on her butt. She kept Alex running, making sure she didn't take a header. She'd climbed over the baby gate so many times Alex had finally removed it for her own safety.

"You're a sight for sore eyes," Ty said, smacking

the side of his leg. Ty had given him a signature Ty
hug earlier at the airport, which involved a lot of
enthusiastic pounding on the back.

"You too."

Bit by bit, he felt himself relax from his long day of
travelling from the Air Force base in Germany to
Eastman, Connecticut. As each of his family members
walked in, he felt that hole in his heart fill a little
more. He'd missed his family. But he'd needed to
prove himself, to be the man Joe had raised him to be.
Joe had taken Park in when he was ten, even offering
to be his foster dad, but Park's mom wouldn't sign the
papers. And the kicker was, Joe had already been a
single dad to six kids. For that, Joe would always have
the honorary title of dad.

"Where's everyone else?" he asked Ty. But what he
really wanted to know was where's Mad? He'd seen her
only a few times over the last ten years and had been
careful to keep his distance. It was the only way to
make the goodbye easier on her. Ty had told him Mad
hadn't handled his leaving well at all the first time,
picking fights and getting in trouble at school. He
didn't want to disrupt her life; he wanted her to be
happy.

"It's too hard on her," Ty had said on Park's first
visit home for Christmas. "She worries about you and
then she gets angry and lashes out in ways that only

end up hurting herself. Keep your distance and it'll help keep her on the right track."

Park swallowed hard. Mad had always been extra special to him. The little pip-squeak he'd missed out on in his own messed-up family. The little sister who lived.

Ty clapped him on the back. "Just until you're home for good. It messes with her head too much otherwise."

Park had reluctantly agreed. He protected her at all costs.

Now Ty was giving him the update on everyone. "Jake's up in Maine with Claire. We'll see him next weekend at the wedding."

Park grunted. Jake was the oldest Campbell and about to marry the movie star Claire Jordan in a private Christmas Eve wedding at her log cabin in Maine. He couldn't wait to hear that story, how Jake snagged the sexiest woman alive.

Ty went on. "Zach's out in no-man's land, completely out of touch, so he won't be here or at the wedding. As usual. Ethan, Ben, Marcus, and Logan should be here any minute." Ty thought for a moment and looked around. "Where's Mad? She was here earlier." He looked to the ceiling and boomed, "Mad, you up there?"

No reply.

"She did all this," Ty said, gesturing to the streamers festively hung all over the room.

"Really?" Park asked, surprised. He couldn't really see Mad doing decorating stuff.

"She's got this book club of women friends now," Ty said with a smirk. "They read smutty books. They must've helped her out. I don't think she would do such a good job by herself. You know Mad."

Park inclined his head. Yeah, he did know Mad. At least he used to. Now that he was home for good, he wanted to be part of her life again. Nerves thrummed through him. "You want to shoot some hoops?"

Ty gave him a sideways look. "It's freezing."

Okay, it was mid-December, but the beer wasn't cutting it for the jumpy feeling in his stomach, the prickly feeling along his legs that made him want to run hard just to get the extra energy out.

"Ty," Alex called, "can you watch her for a minute? I need to make a phone call."

"I got it," Park said, volunteering. He was used to looking out for little Mad. Oh, man, that girl had given him heart attacks on a regular basis, fooling around on the stairs, hanging over the top rail, sliding down the banister. He went to the staircase, where Vivian was making the arduous journey to the top, the stairs extra high for her little legs. He scooped her up, and she squealed in delight. She felt so light, which made him nervous, like she was fragile.

"How about an elevator ride?" he asked, putting her in the crook of his arm like she was sitting on a chair.

"Wee!" she squealed.

He made an elevator noise, walking her up the stairs.

"More!" she exclaimed when they reached the top.

He turned and did the elevator back down.

"Who's hungry?" Josh called, setting a platter of appetizers on the coffee table.

"Me!" Vivian hollered.

He set her in front of the food. She reached out with a wide-open hand, but Josh stopped her. "What do you want?" Josh asked, squatting next to her. "Point and I'll put it on your plate."

Park helped himself to bruschetta, pigs in a blanket, and some bacon-wrapped scallops.

"There's more food coming," Josh said as he put some pigs in a blanket on a plate for Vivian. "Dad's warming up some chicken wings, meatballs, and meatloaf. I got all your favorites." Josh straightened and grinned at Park. "Meat."

"Awesome."

The front door opened and the rest of the guys came in all at once. Park set his plate down, a smile so big it nearly brought tears to his eyes at the sight of his brothers. Logan Campbell, the brother only a year older than Park, and his blood brothers, the kids like him from troubled homes that had found each other through the Police Athletic League.

"Where the hell you been?" Park barked, clapping Logan on the back.

"Where the hell *I've* been?" Logan fired back. "Where *you* been?"

Ethan Case saluted him with a small smirk. "Serving our country. We thank you for your service."

Park socked Ethan in the stomach and met hard muscle. "Damn, you been working out."

"Comes with the territory," Ethan said. He was a cop like Joe, who'd taken them all under his wing.

He greeted Ben and Marcus with similar hug handshakes, his eyes tearing up. He hadn't realized how much he'd missed everyone.

They all stood there just staring at each other for a minute. The faces so familiar and yet different. Even in just the two years since he'd last seen them, they'd changed. Their faces showed the years of hard experience, yet there was some bone-deep part of him that knew them all the way through like only lifelong friends could.

He stepped out of their way. "Come in, there's lots to eat."

"Damn, they went all out for you," Ethan said,

taking in the decorations and the spread on the table.

His dad came in. "Hey, guys, come back to the kitchen. There's way too much food for the coffee table."

They gathered in there, where Alex already sat with Vivian. The little girl was in a high chair for her meal, half of which she tossed on the floor when her daddy wasn't looking. A dog would really clean up around here. He joined in the shared stories, the teasing and joking, but some part of him kept listening for the front door. Where was Mad? What was taking her so long? Was she okay?

An hour later, they moved out of the kitchen, spilling into the living room, beers in hand. Someone turned on the TV to some off-season sports talk. His mind was stuck on Mad. How could she miss his homecoming party? Did it mean nothing that he was home for good? He kept careening from anger that she hadn't bothered to show to primal heart-wrenching fear that something had kept her away. That she was hurt or dead. Like his baby sister. Dead and gone and not a damn thing he could do about it.

He was about to suck it up and text her when the front door sprang open. Mad. He nearly swayed with relief to see her all in one piece. He didn't have to go nuts rescuing her from a too-high tree limb or from instigating a fight she couldn't win or whatever the hell else predicament she got herself in.

She was exactly as he remembered, her petite body swimming in a T-shirt, cargo shorts, and black work boots. Except her hair was dyed red and mussed in a casual way. Last time it had been purple and short.

He set his beer down, about to cross to her for a hug, when she put her hands on her hips and took them all in. "Ta-dah! My grand entrance!" She frowned and muttered, "I need my jeans," before stomping over to the stairs.

"Mad, are you drunk?" Josh asked.

"Park's here," Ty said.

Park crossed to the stairs, where she was already halfway up. "Hey, little bit."

She whirled, her brown eyes flashing. "The virginity train left the station!"

He didn't blink at the odd statement. She was clearly drunk and not making any sense. He'd get some coffee in her. "Tell me you didn't drive yourself home."

She lifted her chin. "I got a ride."

"C'mere."

"I need my jeans," she insisted. He couldn't read her. Her eyes said she was happy to see him, the rest of her seemed pissed off, or maybe she was just that drunk.

"I need a welcome-back hug." He needed it more

from her than any of his brothers. He needed to feel her whole, healthy, alive.

She rolled her eyes, muttered something that sounded like *little twit*, which also made no sense, and then made her way unsteadily down the stairs. She stood in front of him with a belligerent expression.

He wrapped her in a bear hug, kissed the top of her head and ruffled her hair. She scowled and quickly smoothed her hair, which still stuck out on one side. "Good to see ya, mini. Get your jeans and then we're going to sober you up before you say something really stupid."

"Mini?" she barked.

He smiled, remembering how she got huffy about the strangest things. You'd think she would've taken offense to him pointing out she was saying stupid-drunk things. "Sorry, I meant Mad."

She whirled and headed upstairs. He let out a breath and joined his brothers. He was finally truly home.

CHAPTER FOUR

Mad trudged downstairs the next morning in her ratty old T-shirt and sweats, a little hungover, hoping she didn't run into Park. He'd always been a morning person. And she was not. She had just enough headache to remind her what a dumbass she was, getting drunk before the party. She hardly ever got drunk. Some impression she must've made last night.

As she got closer to the kitchen, the scent of fresh-brewed coffee reached her. Her heart kicked up. Had to be Park. Her dad would still be sleeping, he was used to sleeping late after working the night shift as a security guard. He was retired, but still worked part-time for a little extra cash. All of her older brothers had places of their own now.

And then she saw him. Park leaning against the counter, steaming cup of coffee in hand. The slant of sunbeam through the kitchen window lit him in profile. Gorgeous as ever, even more so now that he was older. She'd clearly been fooling herself that the attraction would've died. She took a moment to appreciate the view of short dark hair, sharp cheekbones, square jaw with a couple days' worth of stubble, sexy curve of his lips, and the easy grace of a man comfortable in his own skin.

She stepped into the kitchen.

"Morning," he said. "Coffee?"

"Yes."

He poured her a mug and gave it to her.

"Bless you," she said. It was black, nothing added. Perfect. She sipped. "You doctored it just right."

He grinned. "I didn't do anything. Figured you'd need it straight up. I couldn't get you to drink any last night."

She'd spent the rest of the party eating and trading insults with the guys. What she hadn't done was show Park that she was an attractive sexy woman. Not that it would've mattered. Park had barely glanced at her, too busy yukking it up with the guys. Just like old times.

Get lost, twerp.

Scram, shortstack.

Shut it, mini.

C'mere, little bit, you're on my team. Her dream guy. Was it any wonder she'd worshipped him?

She stifled a groan. She probably looked as crappy as she felt, which sucked after all the fuss she'd made last night with Charlotte's stupid lipstick and her ridiculous attempt to look sexy in jeans. At least she'd brushed her teeth.

Park gave her a sideways look. "How's your head?"

She slowly moved to the round oak kitchen table and sat down. "Shitty."

He reached into the cabinet, pulled out the Advil, and set it in front of her. After all this time he remembered her dad kept headache medicine in a kitchen cabinet. He got her a glass of water too. She tossed a couple back.

"You tie one on a lot?" he asked casually, grabbing the bread and putting four slices in the toaster.

"No," she admitted. She knew he was touchy about that sort of thing because of his crappy parents. And then in case he thought it was because of him, she added, "Just out partying with my friends to celebrate the semester ending." She still had a week of final exams to get through, which meant no more drinking.

"You're still in school?" he asked. "I thought you got your associate's degree last May."

"I did. Now I'm at UConn with a marketing major." The University of Connecticut (UConn) was a little more than an hour commute from Eastman.

He stared at her for a long moment.

"That's why I haven't been in touch as much," she blurted. "Between work and school—"

"No problem."

A few minutes later, he joined her at the table with buttered toast stacked on a plate. He took one for himself and gestured for her to do the same.

They had breakfast in silence. No one in her house ever talked much over breakfast. By the time she finished her coffee, her head was feeling a lot better. Enough for her to test the waters a bit with Park.

"Looks like we'll be roomies again," she said, watching him closely. "Pretty close quarters around here. Our rooms are right across the hall." Her dad had moved back to the master bedroom at the far end of the hallway once her brothers moved out.

He stilled. "You live here? I thought you just crashed last night because you were in no shape to drive."

"I moved back home to save money for college."

"That's awesome you're going for your bachelor's." He gave her a stern look. "Though I'd hoped you'd do that right after high school. What happened?"

You happened.

She raised one shoulder up and down. She'd been devastated when he'd left, listless and anxious, worrying about Park as he moved in and out of war zones, sticking close to the planes that were often first to arrive on the scene. He was flying crew chief, a top mechanic trusted with the most sophisticated of machinery, and the pilots needed him close by to keep the planes in perfect running order. Her anxiety had turned to anger sparking out everywhere. She'd picked a lot of fights, got herself in trouble at school and generally been a teenaged hellion. She couldn't put all the blame at Park's door. She'd always been a bit reckless, more so through the rocky teen years as her brothers left home and she found herself alone too much with too much unfocused energy. Ty got her into his dojo her senior year on one of his visits home. She got strong and focused, but not for the easy path. No, she made things hard on herself, testing herself, taking up bartending in a seedy section of New York City, taking a cheap apartment that was frequently broken in to. She needed to prove she could stand on her own two feet after having the overprotective brother treatment her entire life.

Only recently, a couple of years ago, she'd finally gotten tired of her life, feeling like she was stuck in a rut. Josh had helped her, bringing her back home, getting her a job in the much safer town of Clover Park. Even helping her get the paperwork together to get started at community college.

"Mad, what happened to you?"

"Just took a different path is all," she said, tracing a small circle on the table.

"Well, you're doing great now. I'm proud of you."

She huffed.

"What?"

She stood. "Stop acting like my dad."

"I'm not. I'm your bro." He lifted a fist for a fist bump. Like she was just one of the guys. The guys always called each other bro, whether or not they were related.

She scowled and left him hanging. "None of my bros say shit like that."

"They should."

Her throat felt tight. It really and truly sucked to find yourself still in love with a man who had no feeling for you whatsoever. Except for the stupid friend feeling. No one had ever measured up to the bar he set. And that wasn't because of sex either, because they'd never had anything but a kiss. It was just the good man he was. Despite everything that had happened to him, he'd reached down deep and found some inner strength that touched everything he did with kindness. He'd always been so good to her. Why couldn't he see she was all grown up now? Ready for more?

"Thanks for breakfast," she said and left, heading upstairs for a shower. Her swirling emotions quickly turned to anger. Honestly, what did she have to do to shed the twerpy one-of-the-guys image? Get naked?

She stopped dead in her tracks. It was a ballsy

move, but what the hell did she have to lose? She'd be naked in the shower. Maybe she'd drop the soap or run out of shampoo or need a towel. Something to get him in there. The shower had a frosted glass door, which should show her off in a flattering way. She was fairly sure he wouldn't be able to make out her tattoo clearly through the glass. If he ever did see it, that meant he'd be close enough to touch and at that point there would be no talking.

As soon as she got to the bathroom, she grabbed the two towels hanging in there, hers and her dad's, and tossed them in the hamper. She'd ask for a towel. She took a long shower, relaxing and letting it melt the last of her tension away. Then she scrubbed down, washed her hair, and even shaved her legs. Yup, Park was going to get an eyeful and hopefully a handful. She didn't worry about waking up her dad down the hall. He slept with a white-noise machine, door closed, furthest from the bathroom, and wouldn't be up until early afternoon.

She turned off the shower and poked her head out the shower door. "Park! I need help!"

She wasn't surprised to hear him hustling up the steps only a moment later. He'd always been her hero. Had always rescued her when she got herself in over her head. She shut the shower door and waited for the magic moment when Park's eyes would open to her womanly reality.

He spoke through the bathroom door. "What's wrong? Are you hurt?"

"No. I forgot my towel. Can you get me one?"

"Mad! I thought it was serious. Get your own damn towel."

"In the hall closet."

"I know where the towels are," he said, his voice already fading as he went to fetch one.

The bathroom door opened, and she held her breath, and then scowled.

His hand was over his eyes as he held out the towel. "Here."

She opened the shower door a small amount and held out her hand. "I can't reach it," she said, making no effort whatsoever.

He stepped a little closer, still covering his eyes. "Take it," he ordered, waving it around.

She reached out, took it, and promptly dropped it. "Oops. I dropped it." She lowered her voice to what she hoped was a husky enticing tone. "Everything is so *wet* and *slippery* in here. Can you get it?"

He had to open his eyes to see where it went. He had to see her now. *Come on, come on.*

He turned his back to her, squatted down and reached back for the towel.

Really?

He got it, stood, and turned, eyes closed. "Last chance and then you're on your own. Catch." He tossed it in an arc over the shower door, where it landed on her head. "See ya."

"See ya," she muttered, pulling the towel off her head and drying off. *Fuck my life.*

She adjusted the towel high enough to cover the tattoo over her heart, headed down the hall, and promptly ran into Park. He did a weird careening dance, palms up, to avoid her. She could probably drop the towel right now and he'd just say, "You dropped your towel," and hand it to her.

She seethed and continued to her room.

She was truly grown up now, not a wannabe grown-up at fifteen like she'd been. Dammit. She quickly dressed.

Mad didn't know what made her drive to Hailey's apartment, when she should be holed up in her room, studying for final exams, but here she was. She pressed the bell on Hailey's basement apartment and waited. She knew Hailey normally took wedding planner appointments at the Ludbury House mansion in Clover Park on Sundays, but it was a week before Christmas and she'd closed shop for the holidays.

Hailey opened the door and beamed her dazzling smile, pale blue eyes bright. She wore a pink fuzzy sweater with pink pants, looking all perfectly made up, even for a Sunday at home. "I knew I'd hear from you today. Come in and tell me everything."

Mad stepped inside the cozy little space filled with all sorts of girly stuff—a floral sofa, wood end tables, lamps with little fringes on the shades, romance novels and wedding magazines on display in a bookcase and on the coffee table. Hailey was an unabashed romantic. As a wedding planner should be.

Mad flopped on the super-cushy sofa and sighed. "Nothing to tell. Park still thinks of me as one of the guys."

Hailey cleared a space on the coffee table in front of Mad and slid a coaster there. "Did you wear your black skinny jeans like Charlotte told you to?" The women had all discussed her outfit at the bar, knowing what little she had in her closet.

"Yes!" she barked.

"Lemonade, tea, or water?" Hailey inquired.

"You don't have to get me anything. I don't even know why I'm here. I should be studying. I have a stats final tomorrow."

"Sounds like tea," Hailey said, heading to the nearby kitchen. Her apartment was pretty nice, a living room open to a small dining area and kitchen, a bedroom, and a tiny bathroom. It was the lower level of a colonial home owned by a single career woman, who was rarely home.

Mad followed her into the kitchen.

Hailey set a teakettle on the stove top. "Now what makes you think he sees you as one of the guys?"

"He called me little bit and mini. I'm sure I would've heard shortstack if he'd paid more attention to me than my brothers."

"But that's cute."

"No, he's got me in the friend category. I know when I'm in the friend zone with a guy, believe me." She was too mortified to share that Park had zero reaction to her in nothing but a towel.

Hailey gave her a sympathetic look. "I guess you of all people would know since you have so many guy friends. Gosh, I'm so sorry."

Now Mad felt even worse. Hailey was a die-hard romantic. Even *she* knew there was no hope.

"But don't worry!" Hailey caroled, back to her normally cheerful determined demeanor. "I've got your back. This is no problem."

"How is it not a problem?"

Hailey unveiled a plate of freshly baked chocolate chip cookies and Mad nearly cried. They were her favorite, they were effing delicious, and she just knew Hailey had made them special for her, knowing she'd need to talk today after she was so worked up over Park yesterday. She was so damn thoughtful that way.

"Cookie?" Hailey asked.

Mad pressed her lips tightly together. *I will not cry, I will not cry. I'm tough. I'm strong. I'm fierce.*

Hailey set three cookies on a small plate in front of Mad and then turned to the cabinet for some teacups, pretending not to notice Mad was on the verge of tears.

"Who the fuck needs men anyway," Mad snarled.

"Amen, sister," Hailey said, reaching for the tea bags.

Mad warmed to the topic. "I mean, why make a big effort when all they care about is big tits anyway?"

"Preaching to the choir," Hailey said.

Mad couldn't help but laugh because Hailey actually had big tits. But Hailey had so much more going for her than her looks. She was so damn skilled at the subtle art of conversation, of flirting, of just about everything when it came to social situations. She could even reach Mad where she was, pissed off and frustrated. She wished some of Hailey's people skills would rub off on her.

Hailey grinned and leaned against the counter. "I can't wait to meet him at the wedding." They'd all be heading up to Maine next weekend for her older brother Jake's wedding to an honorary book club member, the actress Claire Jordan. Claire was pretty down to earth once you got to know her. Jake had planned the wedding around when Park could be there.

"Why do you want to meet him so much?" Mad asked.

Hailey shook her head and smiled. "Silly! Of course I want to meet the guy who got you so worked up. He must really be something."

He was *everything*.

Mad shoved a cookie in her mouth so she wouldn't blurt out her pathetically lovesick thoughts. Pure pleasure shot through her at the first bite of cookie—the perfect melt of sugary goodness and chocolate. Josh should have this recipe. Her brother was a foodie and planned to open his own bar with awesome food one day. This should definitely be on the dessert menu. Of course, Hailey would sooner die than share her recipes with Josh.

"This is fucking delicious," Mad said, snagging another cookie. "Never give Josh your recipe. He doesn't deserve it."

"Why would I?" Hailey said, stiffening as she always did when Josh came up. "He can eat a ghost pepper for all I care." That was a really spicy pepper that Josh had slipped into Hailey's nacho appetizer at Garner's once. Hailey had pretended it was delicious— nose red, eyes tearing—and asked for the recipe (over much coughing) to prepare it at home. She was super slick that way. Mad had nearly bust a gut trying not to laugh. Josh had laughed heartily.

Hailey picked up a cookie. "Maybe I'll slip something into a cookie and offer it to him." She took a bite and grinned, chocolate stuck to her super-white front teeth. "Like a bug."

Mad laughed, finding the perfect beauty of Hailey easier to take when there were occasional flaws. "Do it. I'll tell him how awesome they are and then we'll watch him pretend he really enjoys eating bugs."

Hailey wiggled her pointer finger in the air, her way of saying *good plan* without being so rude as to speak with food in her mouth. She finished chewing and swallowed. "Can I make a suggestion?"

The hair on the back of her neck stood up. She just knew she wasn't going to like whatever came out of Hailey's mouth next. She opened her mouth to say no when Hailey popped another cookie in Mad's mouth and grinned.

Mad chewed, too full of chocolately goodness to protest.

Hailey smiled sweetly. "Let's do a makeover for the wedding so you can make a big splash. Makeup, hair, dress with heels, the whole deal. None of this lipstick and skinny jeans half-assed stuff. We want you to look amazing. A woman that Parker can't take his eyes off."

"We?" she asked around the cookie.

Hailey dabbed at her mouth with a napkin. "Yes,

me and the book club ladies. It's your turn for a happy ending."

The teakettle whistled, startling her. *Her turn?* Their book club was dubbed the Happy Endings Book Club on account of it being a romance book club. She thought it meant the happy ending in those books. Hailey actually thought it meant the members' happy endings? Well, their newest member, Claire Jordan, did have a happy ending when she fell in love with Mad's brother Jake. Hailey had arranged the blind date that got them together in the first place. Did Hailey have that kind of power?

"You can't just make a happy ending happen," Mad pointed out, even though she fervently hoped she was wrong. She wanted Hailey to be a miracle worker.

"Tell that to Claire," Hailey replied, pouring hot water into their cups.

"I wore makeup last night," Mad said. "And my skinny jeans. Park was not impressed. This morning he saw me in a towel, practically naked and wet from the shower. And you know what I got? Nothing. He didn't even try to peek at my boobs."

Hailey set tea bags into the cups and turned. "If you trust me with this, let me work my magic, I promise this will be a life-changing weekend. We'll get you in a slutty dress. You can wear those Jimmy Choos that Claire gave you. Every guy will want you. And then we'll launch you at Park. He won't know what hit him."

"Nearly every guy there will be my brother."

Hailey tsked. "No, there's Park, Frank, and Claire's brother, Rich." Frank was Claire's bodyguard, former Army Special Forces. Shaved head, huge muscles, and, okay, yes, Frank was hot, but he was all business on duty. The man never even cracked a smile. Mad could just see herself pushing that stoic guy too far and then he'd snap. *Blam*. Mad kissing the floor, her wrists in cuffs behind her back.

Mad snorted. "Now you're reaching."

"What? Frank's hot. I'm sure Claire's brother will be cute." Hailey carried their teacups to the living room. "Bring the cookies."

Mad grabbed the platter and a handful of napkins from the holder on the dining room table and joined her on the sofa. Her stomach was doing a weird jittery thing. "Forget it. No amount of makeup or slutty clothes will change the fact that Park sees me as anything but a mouthy twerp. Besides, you know I hate dresses. They're uncomfortable and I feel all stiff and weird in them."

"Please," Hailey begged. "Let me do my thing. I just know it'll work. At the very least, it'll give you some confidence."

Mad snagged a cookie. "I have plenty of

confidence. I can kick anyone's ass. No one messes with me." She shoved the entire cookie in her mouth and chewed.

Hailey sipped her tea delicately. "No one is questioning your badassery. Have I ever steered you wrong?"

Mad thought back to the very first time she'd met Hailey, showing up at her singles book club after Josh suckered her into it with a bad bet. She'd thought it was the worst idea ever to go to book club. She didn't even read much back then, but Hailey had welcomed her despite Mad's *I wish I was anywhere but here* attitude, and ultimately won her over with a combination of superhot erotic romance selections and her unwavering faith that they could be friends. Hailey had even tried to learn about sports for Mad, showing up at Mad's Saturday basketball game and playing terribly in front of all the guys. Mad had never fit in with a group of women in her life. Hailey had made that happen.

"Fine," Mad barked. "I'll wear the slutty shoes, but I'm still wearing my pants suit to the wedding." She wasn't even in the wedding party. That was just Josh and Hailey, the two responsible for Jake and Claire meeting. Hailey because she'd set up the blind date and Josh because he'd switched places with his identical twin and Jake went on the date with Claire for him.

"Hair?" Hailey asked.

She shoved a hand in her unruly hair. It was growing out from a short, spiky cut and awkward as hell. "All right, but it stays red."

Hailey nudged her gently in the ribs. "Makeup?"

"If it makes you happy," Mad huffed, rolling her eyes. She hid a smile by slurping her tea, feeling a little secretly hopeful. She sucked at all that girly stuff. And Hailey was practically an expert. She'd done the whole beauty pageant circuit as a teen and won a bunch of them.

"Gracious as ever, Mad," Hailey said. "You'll be kissing my feet with gratitude by the time the weekend is over."

"You wish!"

"This is going to be so fun!" Hailey exclaimed. Her smile dropped suddenly. "It'll be good for me to focus on you. I'm a little nervous about the wedding."

"Why?" It wasn't like Hailey was planning it. She just had to show up.

"I guess I should say I'm nervous about leaving for the wedding. There's been some break-ins in town and Ludbury House doesn't have a security system."

"Really?" she asked, shocked. Clover Park had a very low crime rate. "Are the police going to keep an eye on it for you?"

Hailey folded her hands tightly together in her lap. "Yes. They're cruising the downtown area regularly, keeping a close eye on the situation. I just worry. Ludbury House is the cornerstone of my business—the ceremony, the reception, even my office are all there." Ludbury House was a historic mansion owned by the town of Clover Park. The two-and-a-half-story white clapboard house was impressive with white columns and a wraparound porch. The inside was even more impressive with crystal chandeliers, a grand staircase, and antique furniture that was original to the house.

"Don't worry," Mad said reassuringly. "Chief O'Hare will have the situation locked down tight. You just focus on my makeover."

That got Hailey right back into happy-helper mode. Mad wasn't worried at all. The local police were excellent.

By the time Mad left, she was torn between hopeful and nervous about the makeover. Because if all of Hailey's best efforts failed, Mad had to face facts—Parker Shaw would never be hers.

CHAPTER FIVE

Park was up at the crack of dawn as usual and headed to the resort's gym. He and Ty had arrived last night to the fancy resort in Maine where Jake and Claire's guests were staying all expenses paid. In fact, Jake and Claire were so loaded from their respective businesses—Jake a global tech CEO and Claire a movie star with her own production company—that the entire ocean-side resort had been booked just for the wedding. A full staff was on hand, though most of the rooms were empty. Claire needed privacy for her wedding. The actual ceremony would be tomorrow on Christmas Eve at her log cabin, which he'd heard was huge, and the reception would be in the ballroom of the resort.

He pulled open the glass door of a well-stocked workout room with weights, elliptical machines, treadmills, and stationary bikes. The morning news blared from a few wall-mounted TVs in front of the treadmills, but all he could see was the petite woman running on a treadmill in a midriff top that was little more than a bra and tiny shorts, skin glistening with sweat. Mad. He quickly averted his eyes, crossed to the small counter where a guy in the hotel staff shirt stood, and signed in.

He rolled his neck, considering his options. Just about any piece of equipment was going to put her in his line of vision. How many guys saw her working out like that?

Get to work, he told himself. *It's just Mad.* That shouldn't deter him from his usual morning run. He'd say hi, set the treadmill for a hard run, and watch TV.

He strolled over, casual as could be, as if he had no problem working out next to a nearly naked Mad. He got on the treadmill next to her. "Hey, little bit."

Her head whipped toward him. "Hey, little twit." She didn't break stride, a perfect runner.

"Little twit?" he asked, pressing the button for his warm-up. He started running at a slow pace. "What's that supposed to mean?"

"Whadda ya think?"

Nothing good. He turned to the TV and did his warm-up run, but he couldn't focus on the news. He kept catching glimpses of slick skin moving in perfect athletic strides next to him.

What the hell was she even doing here? She'd

never been a morning person. He cranked up the speed a notch and glanced at her. Her hair stuck out in back like a bad case of bed head and he had the strangest urge to grip that mass of hair in his hand.

"What're you doing up so early?" he asked in a harsh tone because she was screwing up his focus.

"I couldn't sleep," she said, not even out of breath.

He grunted and fixed his eyes on the TV, feeling unreasonably irritated. He worked out all the time with other people, men and women. He just needed to work harder. He cranked up the speed on the treadmill.

She cranked up her speed.

He glanced over at her. She raised a brow in challenge.

He cranked it up again.

She cranked hers up again.

They ran full out in a race to nowhere. His heart pumping, breathing hard, making him feel fully charged, awake and alive.

She finally slowed it down with a laugh. "Too bad—" she huffed and puffed "—it's too cold out for a real race."

He slowed down a notch, still running at a good pace. "You think you could beat me? My legs are still longer." He was five foot eleven to her little bitty size. She'd always wanted to race the guys, and she never won. Not her fault, really. She had to put twice as much into it because of her size disadvantage.

"I could beat you and any of the guys," she returned, doing a cool-down run. "Now you all are old and tired, and I'm still young." She slowed to a walk and grinned. "Finally pays to be the youngest. Twenty-six last week, and I'm not even at my peak."

"Happy belated birthday," he murmured as it hit him that her twenty-six wasn't much different than his twenty-eight. In his mind, she was always much younger. They were two and a half years apart. Sometimes, growing up, like when he was ten to her seven for half the year, he'd lorded it over her, treating her like a little kid. He'd done that every time he'd hit the bigger number until she hit fifteen and things got weird.

"You didn't miss my birthday," she said. "You texted."

"Yeah," he mumbled.

"What?"

He slowed his treadmill, a little dazed. "I just can't believe you're twenty-six now."

She stopped her treadmill and wiped her face with a towel, tossing it over her shoulder. "Old enough for a lot of things I wasn't legal for when you left."

His gaze snapped to hers. "What's that supposed to mean?" He didn't want her touching drugs. Not that they were legal. He barely tolerated her touching alcohol. His family history made him jumpy as hell at the thought.

She grinned and he had a flash of a gap-toothed little-kid Mad grinning down at him from the top of the stairs just before hitching a leg over the railing and sliding down. He'd spent half his life terrified for her safety.

"Wouldn't you like to know?" she asked.

He wanted to interrogate her and then slap on a lecture, but she walked away, hips swinging with attitude, to the weight machine in the corner of the room. He could see her in his peripheral vision. He focused on his workout, running just a little bit harder every time he caught himself watching her work out— her arms, her abs, her legs, everything was smooth, toned, and strong.

That should reassure him. She was fine. Healthy, strong, resilient.

He ran harder.

Finally he finished up and stepped off the treadmill. He turned to find Mad standing there, waiting for him, her skin glowing with good health. He focused on her brown eyes dancing with mischief just like he remembered.

"You want to grab breakfast after we shower?" she asked.

His mind flashed to Mad in the shower last week, asking for a towel and then standing in nothing but a towel out in the hallway. He shut that memory down quick. He'd been relieved not to see her much around the house after that, as she'd spent nearly all her time at the university, studying and taking final exams.

His voice came out harsh. "With you?"

She looked around the workout room, which only had the guy who worked there, standing behind the counter. "Who else?"

He was feeling really weird, a little out of his head. He must've worked out too hard.

She waved a hand in his face. "Are you okay?"

He shook his head. "Yeah, give me twenty minutes."

"What are you, a girl? Ten." She headed to the women's locker room to the right.

He barked out a laugh. Still busting his chops. He turned and went to the men's locker room. See, Mad hadn't changed all that much, he reassured himself.

When he stepped out into the hallway just outside the workout room, Mad was already there, waiting for him. Her hair was still wet from the shower and slicked back, drawing attention to the delicate features of her face—her soft brown eyes, the curve of her cheek, that mouth with the full lower lip. She smelled like something citrusy, sharp and fresh. She wore a

ripped black shirt that exposed her delicate collarbones, cargo shorts, and black work boots. The
contrast of feminine and tomboy reminded him so
much of the girl he remembered, fifteen-year-old Mad
just beginning to show signs of a knockout beauty, a
curvy body hiding under baggy boyish clothes. He'd
tried not to notice back then. He wished he didn't
notice now.

"Come on," she said. "The hotel restaurant is just
around the corner."

He followed her, stealing sideway glances at her,
trying to reconcile his memory of her with the woman
she was today. "You haven't changed much."

She pursed her lips. "Gee, thanks."

"I mean, you were about this size at fifteen."

She grimaced. "I was this size at twelve. Haven't
grown an inch since."

No, she hadn't grown taller, but she'd filled out.
Don't think about it.

"You always wear skimpy workout clothes?" he
blurted.

She eyed him. "Everyone serious about working
out wears the right clothes. Baggy stuff would get
caught on the equipment."

"It looked like you were only wearing—" he
gestured in the general area of her chest "—a, uh, you
know, a, um, bikini top or something."

"A bra?" she asked way too loud. "Is that what you can't say? A bra?"

"Shh." His neck was hot, the tips of his ears too. Mad enjoyed messing with people. And the more she could make them squirm, the better. He couldn't let her know she'd gotten to him. "Yeah, a bra."

She shoved his shoulder. "You try shopping in the women's fitness department. It's all sports bras and half tops. The men's stuff is way too big for me."

He kept his mouth shut. He shouldn't have brought it up. What did it matter if she wore skimpy stuff at the gym? Probably lots of women did. Just because he was noticing her didn't mean she was *trying* to draw extra attention to herself.

They got to the restaurant and the waitress gestured for them to take a seat. They were the first customers. Mad went to a table for two by the window with a view of the ocean. The sky was gray; the water a bluish-gray. Maine in winter. It made you want to sit in front of a roaring fire.

He sat across from her. "Don't you want to dry your hair? It's freezing."

She scrunched her hands in her hair, making it stick up. He wondered if those spikes were soft. "I didn't have a hair dryer."

He gestured for the waitress and ordered them two coffees. Then he pulled off his gray sweatshirt and handed it to her. "Put it on." He had a T-shirt under it.

She crossed her arms. "I'm fine. Besides, you'll be cold without it."

He shook the sweatshirt at her. "I'm cold just looking at you."

"Then don't look at me."

"Put the damn shirt on."

"No."

He set the shirt on the side of the table and crossed his arms. She stared at his biceps. "Then we'll both be cold."

She lifted her chin. "I'm not cold at all."

He heaved an exasperated breath and put the sweatshirt over the back of his chair. "So damn stubborn."

"So damn overprotective," she returned. "I don't need a protector. I could kick your ass." Her brown eyes glittered in challenge. She was all sass and attitude, exactly like he remembered. He relaxed a bit, feeling on more stable ground now that they were both fully dressed and bantering like old times.

"Ya think?" He laughed. "I've got a good sixty pounds of muscle on you."

"Say the word," she said with a smile that was downright scary. "I can't wait to see you go down."

He jolted. *She didn't mean that dirty, right?*

The coffee arrived. Thank God. He took a sip, leaving it black. "Sweet as always, Mad."

She sipped her coffee too, taking it at its full bitter strength like he did. "I wasn't raised to be sweet and pretty."

"No, you were not." She was raised in a houseful of males, who she imitated, doing her best to fit in with them all.

She scowled.

"Don't pout, shortstack. Sweet is overrated."

She brightened. "So what's the plan now that you're home? You have any job prospects lined up?"

He warmed his hands on the mug. "Nothing definite. After the holidays, I'll apply to a bunch of airlines, maybe Boeing out in Seattle. Someone must need a mechanic."

"So you're leaving again?"

"I dunno. We'll see what pans out. I've got some savings, so I'll be okay for a few months."

"Oh."

"What?"

She shook her head and tufts of red hair bounced, already drying a little. "I guess I just thought when you came home, you'd be home for good."

"I gotta work."

"Yeah, I know."

Now why did she sound so glum? Before he could

ask, the waitress returned to take their order. They both ordered omelets. He asked her about college, and she told him about her marketing and advertising major and how interesting her classes were. He was thrilled to hear she was getting her degree. She'd always been sharp.

"So what took you so long to get to college?" he asked just as the food arrived. "Why were you bartending?"

She dug into her food. "Paid the rent."

"I still don't get why you waited for school. You had the grades. You could've been well into a career by now."

She set her fork down with a clatter. "Ya know, I'm really getting sick of the way you talk down to me."

He was taken aback. "I don't talk down to you."

"Yes, you do. Like you still think I'm a kid. Like when you left."

"I know you're not a kid." He shoved some omelet in his mouth. He knew she was all grown up, had gotten a very clear visual on that, thank you very much. He chewed ferociously. But she was still his to protect. Now that he was home, he'd slipped right back into that role.

"Then what am I to you?" she asked.

He glanced at her, caught the glittering challenge

in her eyes, and went back to eating. "You're Mad. Same as always."

"I'm not the same," she said tightly.

He blew out a breath. "What're you getting so pissy about?"

She stabbed her fork in her omelet and sawed off a piece. "I'm not pissy."

"Whatever."

They finished their meal in silence. He had no idea what her problem was. The check arrived, and he pulled out his wallet and set some bills on the table.

"Thank you," she said softly.

"No problem." He tucked his wallet in his jeans pocket. "Ready to go?"

"Park, I have to tell you something."

His gut tightened, already imagining worst-case scenarios. Whatever kind of trouble she was in, he'd fix it.

He leaned forward across the table. "What?"

She bit her lip.

"Just say it," he urged. "I'll take care of it."

She slowly shook her head. "Nothing."

"Come on, it's something."

She stood abruptly. "We should get going."

He stood, concerned and hurt that she wouldn't come to him when she had a problem. She always used to. He'd been away too long.

They walked toward the exit. "Mad, I'm home now. Whatever kind of trouble it is—"

"No trouble. Forget I said anything. Really. I've been hanging with the girls too much." She waved a hand in the air. "Girl-talk stuff. Sharing and caring."

His brows scrunched together in confusion, not quite sure what girl talk had to do with her problem. "Sure?"

"Yup."

When they reached the hallway, he reached over and ruffled her hair. "You change your mind, you know where to find me."

She smoothed her hair and frowned. "See ya tonight," she snarled before jogging off in the opposite direction.

"See ya, mini."

She turned, opened her mouth and shut it, and then turned away without another word. Damn, she was moody. One minute sweet, the next sour. What happened to the girl that used to look at him like he was her hero?

Chapter Six

Mad was spitting mad by the time she and her friends pulled up in a limo to Claire's log cabin for the tree-decorating party later that day. She felt like bopping Park over the head to knock some sense into him. Not even her oldest brothers, twins Jake and Josh, treated her like a little twerp the way Park did. Seriously, look at Josh, who'd helped her get settled at a new job and community college. He was hands off, only occasionally inquiring how she was doing. She knew she could ask him for help if she needed any, but guess what, she didn't! Because she was doing just fine!

"Is that cashmere?" Charlotte asked, feeling the sleeve of Mad's white V-neck sweater.

"Yeah," Mad said. "Hailey found it at the consignment shop, but it made her itch. I don't know why. It's so soft."

"I guess I'm just supersensitive," Hailey chirped from the seat across from her. "It looks cute with your black jeans and boots."

The other women agreed.

"Thanks," Mad muttered. Not that it mattered that she was all dressed up like some kind of Hailey wannabe. Park hadn't given her a second look in her barely there workout clothes.

They stepped outside. The place really shouldn't be called a cabin. It was a sprawling two-story home with six bedrooms and a three-car garage. Only Jake, Claire, Claire's family, and Claire's bodyguard were staying there. Mad glanced around, spying security cameras discreetly placed along the big wraparound porch. Probably more around the place that she couldn't see. They'd passed a few no-trespassing signs nailed to the trees too.

Hailey rang the bell. A man in a tuxedo answered, escorting them in and taking their coats.

She stepped inside the two-story great room with an enormous flagstone fireplace, a tall Christmas tree with white lights in the corner, and several burgundy leather sofas and chairs arranged in front of the roaring fire.

"You're here!" Claire Jordan, the bride-to-be and internationally famous movie star, exclaimed, rushing over to them. Her hair was back to blonde, up in a sophisticated twist, her flawless skin glowing. She wore a cap-sleeved red dress with roses and black lace that gave peeks of the skin underneath. Her bodyguard, Frank, stood nearby, back to the wall, his expression stone.

Hailey got to Claire first and gave her a warm hug.

Claire kissed Hailey's cheek and beamed. "I'm so glad you all could make it!" They'd seen her only a few weeks ago back in LA for the premiere of Claire's movie *Fierce Longing*. They'd all been invited to the red-carpet event both because they were friends with Claire and because they'd all played extras in the corporate party scene.

Claire gave Mad a hug and then squeezed her hands. "Now we'll really be sisters! This time tomorrow night."

Mad got an unexpected lump in her throat. She hadn't really thought of it like that. "I always wanted a sister."

"Me too!" Claire said, beaming her perfect Hollywood smile. If she wasn't such a down-to-earth person, Mad would find her perfect good looks irritating. Claire had managed to hook Jake, even in disguise as a regular girl with no makeup, a red wig, green contacts over her hazel eyes, and no glam clothes at all. She was a natural flawless beauty, but when she glammed it up, she was stunning. The cameras loved her.

Jake strode over in a designer light blue button-down shirt and gray pants. His thick brown hair was freshly cut for the wedding. He smiled at Mad, crinkles forming at the corners of his dark brown eyes. "How's the resort?" he asked, giving her a one-armed hug and ruffling her hair.

She smoothed her hair. Geez, none of her brothers gave a crap about the fact that it took time to make your hair look good. She'd let Hailey put in some anti-frizz stuff. "Stop with the hair. Geez, I'm not nine years old."

"Can't help it," Jake said, putting her in a headlock and rubbing his knuckles across her head. "You're just cute as a little Chihuahua."

She could have him flat on his back in an instant, but didn't want to damage the groom. Instead she gave him a sharp jab to the kidneys, and he released his hold with a soft "oof." He rubbed his side.

"Hey, hey," Claire said, putting up a hand. "I need to get him to the altar tomorrow. You two can kick each other's butt the day after that."

"The perfect Christmas present," Mad replied.

Claire went to greet the rest of their friends. Mad wandered further into the room. Her dad introduced her to Claire's parents and her brother. Nice people. A few moments later, she found her brothers over in the dining room, chowing down on a bunch of cold appetizers. An archway to her left led to a large formal living room with wood paneling, several high-back chairs and a couple of dark blue patterned sofas arranged around a fireplace. She peeked into the huge kitchen to her right and saw staff in there preparing hot food. Then Ty shifted out of the way and her gaze landed on Park looking hot as hell in a black leather jacket over a blue button-down shirt. He met her eyes and quickly turned back to Ty.

Nerves ran through her. She couldn't believe she'd nearly confided she was in love with him over breakfast. All the confiding in her friends had made her nearly blurt everything. Even she knew you couldn't open with the L word. The fact that he'd immediately morphed into avenging protector mode told her she had a long road ahead from little twerp to sexy potential girlfriend. Unfortunately, patience was not her strong suit.

She moved to stand next to Josh in the corner of the room, the most laid-back of her brothers, which made him the easiest to hang out with.

"Hey," she said.

"Hey yourself," Josh said, taking a shrimp and dipping it into cocktail sauce. Josh was the casual version of his identical twin, Jake. He let his thick brown hair grow long enough to curl a bit at the nape of his neck, his jaw was nearly always stubbled with a couple days' growth, and, unlike Jake's designer style,

Josh favored flannel shirts, faded tees, and ripped jeans. Tonight he'd dressed up a bit in a white button-down shirt with black jeans.

"How'd your finals go?" Josh asked.

"Good, I think." She grabbed a small plate and piled it with veggies.

He stopped eating, his dark brown eyes direct. "You study hard?"

"Yes, I studied," she said tightly. "I'm paying half the tuition, I'm not going to blow it off."

Josh said nothing, just kept eating, but she knew she was in the wrong, taking out her aggravation with Park on him.

"Sorry," she said. "I'm still a little wound up from a week of exams. You know I appreciate your contribution."

Josh had covered what she couldn't in the cost of tuition. Her dad didn't have the funds after helping out all of her older siblings. Sometimes being the youngest meant you got the leftovers. Josh had dipped into his savings, postponing his own dream of opening a bar, to help her out. She hadn't even asked him to. They'd sat down together, figured out what she'd need to get her bachelor's degree, he saw where she was short and simply said he'd cover it and wouldn't take no for an answer. She'd argued that Jake was better funded and she'd ask him, but Josh got pissed off at being passed over for his rich twin, so she shut up.

"I expect a complete marketing campaign for my bar," Josh said, pointing a shrimp at her. "This ain't no free ride."

"You got it," she said. "You'll be my first client. As soon as I graduate, you get your bar, and I'll set you up."

"I made an offer on Garner's," Josh said.

"You did?"

"Yeah. Clive said he'd think about it. He's on the fence about retirement." Clive Garner, owner of the bar, was a spry seventy-three. His wife and co-owner, Heather, was sixty-five and anxious for them to retire and travel. The couple had promoted Josh to manager last May when they decided to cut back their hours.

Josh took a sip of water and went on. "I figure it's more affordable to take over Garner's than build something new."

"Wow. I didn't know you had enough saved to make an offer."

"I live pretty frugally." He took another shrimp, chewed, and swallowed. "If I save more, I can afford to expand it. Add on a back room with a dance floor, jukeboxes, a couple pool tables."

"Cool."

He smiled. "Yeah, we'll see. He's not taking offers from anyone else. It's either me or he hangs onto it a little longer."

She inclined her head. She could totally see Josh taking over Garner's and making it his own. He'd worked there for eight years now. "Would you change the name?"

He nodded, a small smile playing over his lips.

"To what?"

"You'll see."

"What's the big secret?" she demanded.

"Drop it," he said.

She did, chomping on a yellow pepper slice. She knew he wouldn't give up any further information. Despite his laid-back persona, he had the heart and mind of a fierce warrior. There was no other word for it. He'd been a paratrooper in the Army, jumping out of planes and engaging the enemy in hand-to-hand combat. He'd been chosen for that unit based on his temperament and physicality, cool and calculating, reserved and strong. He was easygoing, yes, all charming smiles and gentlemanly manners, but he could *not* be pushed.

They ate for a few moments in silence, the noise of their brothers laughing and talking surrounding them. Alex held his daughter, Viv, who wiggled like crazy to get down. He set her down and she raced to the kitchen. Alex took off after her.

"You ever think about getting married?" Mad

asked Josh. She knew he and Jake had a tight twin bond, being identical. She had to wonder if now that Jake was getting married, Josh would want to settle down too.

"Nope," he said.

"Why not?"

"I guess I just like living alone, answering to no one."

"Yeah, I get that," she said. Her gaze drifted to Park, lingering on his square clean-shaven jaw. Here she was living with Park and it was irritating to the extreme. "I could see how that would get old *real* fast."

Hailey appeared at Mad's side. "Hello!" she said brightly and then whispered in Mad's ear, "Where's Park?"

"With Ty," she said as quietly as possible, not wanting Josh to pick up on it. But she didn't have to worry. Josh's eyes were locked on Hailey and his smile was slow and devious.

"Where's my *hello*?" Josh asked, imitating Hailey's perky tone.

"It seems to have disappeared," Hailey said dryly, "just like my cash."

Mad bit back a grin. Hailey and Josh used to have a strange arrangement where he accompanied her to weddings as her date in exchange for cash. After Hailey had called the whole thing off, she'd demanded he return her money. Josh had it stashed in a shoebox in his closet, but was holding out, to Hailey's outrage, until she went to his place and got it herself.

"I told you where it is, princess," Josh drawled. "All you have to do is come and get it." That last part sounded like an invitation to seduction even Mad couldn't miss.

Hailey flushed bright pink and jabbed a finger in Josh's direction. "Hell will freeze over before I step into that den of sin!"

Josh threw back his head and laughed.

Her brothers looked over, curious.

"Come over here, honey," Ty called to Hailey. "I'll treat you better than that scoundrel."

Her brothers laughed.

Mad snorted. That was one of the many old-fashioned names Hailey called Josh. Scoundrel, cad, and beast being her top three. He called her princess. Always. Probably because she was so graceful and smooth from her beauty pageant training.

Hailey grabbed Mad by the elbow and dragged her over to Ty and Park. "Hi, I'm Hailey," she said to Park.

Park gazed at Hailey for a long moment while Mad shrank into the wallpaper. Hailey's beauty had that effect on men. "Parker Shaw, nice to meet you."

Hailey threw an arm over Mad's shoulders. "I

helped Mad get your homecoming party ready. Did you even recognize her when you got home? People change a lot over the years."

Mad felt her cheeks flush. Could Hailey be any more obvious?

Park's gaze landed on her. "Mad hasn't changed one bit."

Her heart cracked into brittle shards as the last little bit of hope inside her died. She was so devastated she couldn't even speak, couldn't move, could only stand there like an idiot.

"Of course she's changed," Hailey said, immediately defending her honor. "You can't tell me she looks like a fifteen-year-old."

Mad shrugged Hailey's arm off her. Next thing you knew, Hailey would be pointing out Mad's boobs.

"Same old mouthy twerp," Ty said around his beer bottle.

Mad finally came back to herself and snapped at Ty. "Why don't you go jump out a window?"

"See?" Ty said, not offended in the least. He was a stunt guy and regularly jumped out of windows.

Park's eyes were half hooded, making her crazy because she couldn't read him anymore.

"Mad might be mouthy," Hailey said, rushing to defend her, "but she's also smart and funny and, and…"

Mad squirmed, mortified that Hailey had run out of positive adjectives. Ty and Park had nothing good to add either. They merely waited for Hailey to come up with something.

"A great athlete!" Hailey finally said triumphantly.

Mad turned away, pretending she had something in her eye. It was nice of Hailey to mention it.

"Park, maybe you should get to know her all over again now that she's a card-carrying adult," Hailey suggested in her oh-so-subtle way.

"What kind of card?" Ty asked with a smile in his voice.

Mad turned back to see both men looking thoroughly entertained by Hailey. "Don't say it," Mad warned. But, of course, Hailey went on proudly.

"A card-carrying member of the Happy Endings Book Club," Hailey announced cheerfully, producing a card from her purse. The card had frigging pink hearts on it and read Happy Endings Book Club. And then under that, "Join the club and get your happy ending!" Mad's card from Hailey was stuffed in the back of her underwear drawer along with the box of condoms she'd bought in hopes of an event that was rapidly becoming an impossibility.

Ty took the card, flipping it around his fingers. "Maybe I'll join." He leaned close to Hailey and leered. "I like happy endings."

"I'd love to help you find your happy ending!" Hailey exclaimed, seeming oblivious to Ty's overture.

Her brothers laughed, except Josh, who turned and left the room.

Ty snagged Hailey's elbow. "Oh, yeah?" He led her away, saying, "Tell me more."

Hailey chattered on happily. She was such a focused wedding planner/matchmaker, so set on building a solid foundation for her business, that she never took the time to find love for herself. She'd explained she would when the time was right. Joke would be on Ty in the end when Hailey tried to set him up.

It was just her and Park. She swallowed, suddenly nervous. Which was just stupid. She shifted back and forth on her feet and was about to bail when he spoke.

"How'd you meet her?"

She shook her head. "Long story."

"She's like the anti-Mad."

She ground her teeth. Like she didn't know how beautiful Hailey was. "Thanks a lot."

He cocked a brow. "I just meant she's, you know, all made up, like…and you're not."

She whirled away because she knew exactly what he meant. Hailey was beautiful and Mad was plain.

Park snagged her by the back of the collar. "Hey, it's not a bad thing."

She turned back to face him, jaw tight. "Whatever."

"Why're you so pissy with me?"

"Why do you think?"

"I don't know. PMS?"

"That's exactly right," she snapped. Men always blamed PMS. God forbid a woman actually have legitimate feelings that needed to be heard. If only she could find the right words.

His hazel eyes narrowed. "I thought you'd be happy to see me, but for some reason all I do is piss you off." He backed away. "I'll leave you alone."

She was about to scream *don't walk away, you idiot*, when someone rang a little bell and called them all to the great room to decorate the tree. She strode over to the great room, joining her friends. Hailey was introducing Ty to supersweet, super-accommodating Lauren, who Ty would absolutely steamroll.

"So nice to meet you, Lauren," Ty said, his smile all cocky confidence. "You into happy endings too?"

Lauren blushed furiously and tucked her long light brown hair behind her ears. "Of course, we all are. Do you enjoy romances?"

Ty leaned close. "Sometimes. Depends on the girl."

"Oh!" Lauren's hand fluttered in the air. "I didn't mean real life. I meant books." She shot Hailey a pleading look, who was oblivious as she scanned the room, probably looking for another couple to get together.

"Everyone grab a box of ornaments," Claire announced. "Put them wherever you like on the tree. Then I have tinsel and Jake's doing the star because he's my star."

The women *awwed* in unison, except Mad, who made a gagging motion, sticking her finger down her throat.

Jake wrapped an arm around Claire's waist, tugging her close and kissing her temple. "You're my star."

"She's everyone's star!" Ty quipped and everyone laughed because it was true. She was the Hollywood elite, a star with her choice of projects, always in the spotlight.

Everyone started decorating. Mad had just gotten to the second box of ornaments, some silver and gold balls, when Hailey whispered, "Put yours up high. It'll make the sweater rise up and show off your skinny waist. He'll notice."

Mad didn't question her friend's expert advice, merely followed it because she was just that desperate and thoroughly screwing things up. She returned to the tree with two ornaments, making sure she was positioned where Park would get an eyeful, and reached up high, stretching her arms until the sweater pulled up enough to show some skin. She did have a nice waist; her daily core workouts should be good for something. Maybe his eyes would catch there and drift lower. Maybe he'd get ideas.

She did it twice, one big stretch for each ornament, and risked a peek over to where he was, diagonally behind her, but his eyes were fixed on her stupid boots. She glanced down to make sure there wasn't a scrap of toilet paper there. Nope. So that was where she stood. She showed off her waist and ass, and Park examined her shoes for no reason whatsoever.

She stifled a sigh and went back to the box of ornaments to report to Hailey that it hadn't worked.

"Oh, it worked," Hailey said. "He definitely noticed. Do it again."

"He did not. He was staring at my shoes."

"Trust me."

She did trust her, so, feeling like a fool, she repeated the whole thing with two more ornaments, this time reaching up and to the right, making an even bigger curvy gesture. She glanced over her shoulder to see Park approaching. Her heart thumped wildly. It worked! He noticed! He was going to do something about it!

"Looks like you could use some help on the high branches, mini," he said, holding his hand out for the next one.

She deflated, handing it to him. "Thanks," she mumbled. She caught Hailey giving her a big thumbs-up. Mad shook her head.

By the end of the night, Mad drooped back to the limo, full of good food, surrounded by close friends, and feeling utterly hopeless.

Hailey sat next to her in the limo and bumped her shoulder. "My offer still stands."

"What offer?" Charlotte asked, stretching out her long legs. "You going to set her up?"

Hailey wiggled in excitement. "We're going to do a Mad makeover for the wedding tomorrow and Park won't know what hit him."

Ally and Carrie squealed. Lauren looked at her curiously.

Mad slumped lower in her seat. "I really don't see the point." Before she'd thought it would work, but now, after Park paid her no mind in a towel, skimpy workout clothes, and a sweater reveal, she had serious doubts.

Charlotte leaned forward and nudged Mad's leg. "Hey." Her brown eyes were warm, her tone reassuring. "Remember Claire's premiere? You were super glammed up then and even Blake Grenier hit on you at the after party." That was the star of Claire's movie *Fierce Longing*.

Mad brightened and sat up. "He did, didn't he?" Not that she wanted to be with gorgeous Blake after he'd been such a jerk to Claire, but he had ignored his supermodel date to flirt with her. Hell, if she could catch the sexiest man alive's eye, maybe she stood a chance.

"But you have to wear a slutty dress," Hailey said, "no pants suit."

Mad frowned. "I'd show up naked if I thought it would work, but the man didn't blink when he saw me with just a towel on."

"Say what?" Charlotte asked.

Mad quickly filled her in.

Charlotte chuckled and gave Mad a high five. "Slick."

"That sounded like a yes to glamming you up," Hailey said with a grin.

Mad laughed. "Okay, yes, have your girly way with me. And if this doesn't work, I'm done with PMS. It's making me damn irritable."

"You have PMS?" Charlotte asked. "Stay away from salty foods." She was a health nut thanks to her job as a personal trainer.

"I meant Parker Michael Shaw," Mad said.

The women burst out laughing. She did too. She'd nearly forgotten how fun his initials were.

"I just know this is going to work!" Hailey

exclaimed. "We just have to open his eyes and make him see you in a different way." She gave Mad a serious look. "And you have got to stop snarling at him. I don't care how frustrated you are. All that snarling just reminds him you used to be a mouthy twerp. We want elegant, sophisticated, cultured."

"I think you want a different girl," Mad muttered.

"Channel Elizabeth Bennet," Hailey counseled. "Park already has the dark and broody Mr. Darcy down pat." That was their most recent read for book club, a classic for the holidays, *Pride and Prejudice*. Mad had to admit that Mr. Darcy was doing more for her than she thought a guy from a hundred years ago could. So broody and romantic.

Mad squirmed a little, part excited, part nervous. But at least that little spark of hope was back.

CHAPTER SEVEN

"Get that thing the hell away from me!" Mad barked as Hailey's metal contraption nearly blinded her. "You said make my eyes pop, not make my eyes pop out!" She knocked the evil thing from Hailey's hand.

Hailey let out a huge sigh. "I told you not to move. You have beautiful eyes. The lash curler will just accentuate them." She retrieved the evil thing.

Mad leaned back. "Sure, he'll notice I'm missing an eye."

Hailey tsked. "Don't be such a baby. Geez. We have a lot more to do and it would help if you cooperated." They were in a large two-bedroom suite at the resort, getting ready for the wedding.

"There's more?" Mad asked, incredulous. She'd already spent an ungodly amount of time getting her hair styled and blown dry. Okay, she had to admit the hairdresser Claire hired worked miracles. There wasn't much you could do with her hair that wasn't quite short and wasn't quite long. But she now sported some cute waves that fell in soft layers. Even her dyed red hair went from shocker to subdued. Maybe she should go natural, back to brunette. Nah. She'd do that once she had to for a job interview or something. She liked bright colors. Maybe next she'd try blue. Or gray.

"Which slutty dress do you like better?" Ally asked, looking way too excited about the two dresses she held up. They were Hailey's dresses, who'd brought at least a dozen with her. One was pink with a plunging neckline and a slit up one leg. It was cool with the slit and all, but pink made her gag. The other dress was black, sleeveless, and short. No-brainer.

She stood and held the black dress up to her, making sure it went high enough to cover her tattoo. She wasn't embarrassed about having a tattoo, she just wasn't ready for Park to see it. Not until things were different between them. After her heart was no longer swinging in the wind, all exposed and vulnerable.

"Perfect!" Hailey exclaimed. "It fits me like a glove. Can't wait to see you in it." She turned to Ally. "Can you get the black lace shawl?"

Mad's brows scrunched together. "What's the point in covering up a slutty dress?"

"Guys need to imagine it coming off," Hailey explained. "It's much sexier to cover up. It'll keep slipping off your shoulder and he'll be dying to peel it off."

That sounded backward. Guys didn't look at covered-up centerfolds. Whatever. Wearing a towel hadn't worked. A frosted glass shower wall hadn't worked. Maybe Hailey was right. The centerfolds *were* hidden in several pages of bogus articles.

Hailey pushed Mad into the chair in front of the vanity table. "Stay still and look up. I'm going in with mascara. We're skipping the lash curler."

"Fine," Mad said, secretly happy that Hailey took over.

When she'd finished, Mad looked in the mirror. Her eyes did look bigger and a deeper shade of brown.

She met Hailey's blue eyes in the mirror. "What do I do once he sees me all made-over?" she asked in a soft voice. She didn't want all the women to chime in. She was embarrassed enough that she even had to ask.

Hailey leaned down, her head right next to Mad's, and smiled at her in the mirror. "Easy. You dance with him."

Mad bit back a groan. "I don't know how to dance. And we don't have time for lessons. Augh. This is never going to work."

Hailey straightened. "Anyone can slow dance. Just put your arms around his neck. He'll do the rest."

Mad stared at the table. "What if he doesn't want to dance?"

"Put your arms around his neck anyway. See what happens."

Mad turned to face Hailey, eager to move the topic away from her own awkwardness. "Did you find anyone else to join your dance with Josh?" Hailey was supposed to dance with Josh for the bridal party dance, though they were the only two in the bridal party, and she'd already informed Josh that it was fine with her if they invited others to join them. She was probably hoping to bail as soon as another couple got on the dance floor. Josh had replied quite seriously, "I could never disappoint the bride's wishes," which Hailey had thought was no kind of answer.

Hailey stiffened. "No."

Mad chuckled.

Hailey glared. "I know you think it's funny that your brother drives me nuts. But for me, well, he's a beast! I can barely stand to be in the same room with him. Do you know he's been missing at least one ingredient for my favorite drink for the past six months? I can never get a decent mojito anymore."

Mad lifted one shoulder up and down. "So go to a different bar."

Hailey tossed her long strawberry blonde hair over one shoulder. "Why should I have to leave my hometown bar just because he's too incompetent a manager to get the proper ingredients?" Her voice got a little enthusiastic on the word manager, like maybe she was secretly happy for his promotion. These two were fucked up.

"You know he's doing it on purpose, right?" Mad asked.

"Of course I know! Because he's a cad. Ever since he's been missing an ingredient, I've been explaining his unfortunate condition." She raised two fingers and then made them droop.

"We know!" Charlotte exclaimed with a laugh. Everyone knew.

Hailey beamed. "The important thing is, *he* doesn't know."

But just wait until he found out, Mad thought. She mentally rubbed her hands together, already imagining what Josh's devious revenge would be.

The women finished getting ready, all made up, hair styled and sprayed, formal dresses in place. Hailey wore a deep red off-the-shoulder satin sheath that clung to her curves, Charlotte looked stunning in a bright yellow asymmetrical dress that exposed one shoulder and was short enough to show off her long legs, and Ally, Carrie, and Lauren all had versions of the little black dress. She supposed she wouldn't stick out as much as she feared in her little black dress.

Mad dressed last, postponing the uncomfortable feeling of wearing a dress until the last possible minute. She turned her back on the women, pulled off her cargo shorts and long-sleeve shirt, and slipped on the dress. It fit her perfectly. Not skin-tight as it would have been on the bustier, curvier Hailey, but it looked good. She hiked up the top, making sure her boobs could hold it in place and her tattoo was covered. There.

She crossed to the full-length mirror set up just for them. Bra had to go. She slipped that off and tossed it on her clothes pile on the floor. She turned to her friends, who were all staring at her. "What?"

"Don't take this the wrong way," Charlotte started.

"Because boy shorts are super cute," Lauren said.

"If you like that style of panty," Ally said, "which some people do." She nodded enthusiastically, making her blond bangs bounce in time.

Mad narrowed her eyes.

"They have to go," Hailey said.

Mad ran a hand over her hip. "What's wrong with them?"

"Lines," Hailey said. "It's ruining the shape of the dress. Bunchy boy shorts."

"They're girl panties," Mad protested.

"I've seen some cute bra-panty sets in that style," Ally said.

The women all rushed to agree.

Hailey shook her head. "But not in that dress."

"But that's the only kind I have!" Mad exclaimed. And she was not going to wear Hailey's preferred thong. It was weird to share underwear.

Hailey looked at her expectantly.

"And I don't have time to shop," Mad added lamely as it dawned on her what the only solution was. "But the dress is so short," she whispered, tugging at the hem as if that would make it longer. It was maybe three inches past her ass.

"Just keep your legs crossed when you sit down," Hailey said.

Charlotte grinned. "And if anyone plays 'New York, New York' at the reception, don't join us in the kick line." They cracked up.

Hailey smiled. "It'll be a nice surprise for Park later."

Hailey's confidence in her ability to hook Park gave Mad a much-needed boost. She wiggled her boy shorts panties off and stepped into the Jimmy Choos, a wedge heel that wasn't too high for her to manage. They were a gift from Claire, who'd given all of them free rein to pick whatever they wanted from her closet of fancy dresses and shoes the night she had to say goodbye after her movie wrapped in Connecticut last year.

The women broke into applause, beaming at her.

Mad's cheeks burned furiously. "Bitches, please!" She snagged the black lace shawl. "Let's blow this popsicle stand."

No one moved.

"Popsicle stand?" Hailey asked.

Mad waved that away. "My dad's rubbing off on me since I moved back home. Let's go."

They left the suite, rode down the elevator all polished and smelling like the floral high-end perfume Claire had left for them, and headed out to the waiting limo. The wedding would be in the great room of Claire's cabin in front of the fireplace, the reception back here at the resort, where a huge ballroom had been decorated in Christmas greenery for the occasion. It would be an easy trip upstairs to Park's room or hers for what she hoped would happen next.

Her friends chatted excitedly on the ride over, seeming perfectly comfortable and happy to have a chance to dress up for a formal occasion, but for Mad it was simply a means to an end. She wanted to wow Park. *This is the Mad you never knew existed. You want some of this? Come and get me!*

~ ~ ~

Mad followed her friends to a row of cushioned chairs second to the front. Hailey took her place in the back with the bride. Jake and Josh were already standing up front by the hearth, looking dashing in black tuxedoes. She knew the moment Park arrived because he was with Ty, who was loud and boisterous as ever. He and Park were close, but Park was the quiet reserved one. He ran deep, whereas Ty let everything hang out.

She was glad to be on the aisle so she could see Claire's approach once the music started. She was sure she'd be stunning in her bridal gown.

Someone tugged her hair and she turned, annoyed. Her brothers were forever messing with her hair. Like she was their little pet.

"Hey, shortstack," Ty said with a grin, standing in the aisle behind her, "heard Santa fell off the roof and broke his neck, so don't expect anything this year."

Park elbowed him and shook his head. He wore a navy blue suit, standing tall, shoulders back as though he were in his formal Air Force uniform. Gorgeous. Her pulse pounded in her ears. Did he notice anything different about her?

"Ha-ha," she returned. Ty always used to tease her as a kid, telling her Santa got in some kind of accident that would prevent him from showing on Christmas. She used to get really mad and yell at him, rushing to her dad for reassurance. Loser.

"Hello, ladies," Ty said, addressing her friends. Park raised a hand in greeting.

"Hi, guys," her friends chorused.

Park and Ty settled behind her. She faced front, a little disappointed that Park's eyes didn't travel any further than her face. Did he notice her eyes were accentuated with mascara? That she wore blush and rose lipstick and who knew what else Hailey had applied. It was all a blur of potions. She swore under her breath. She'd be really pissed if she went through all this effort and he didn't notice anything at all. She tried not to fidget as she heard Ty behind her, talking about his latest movie that had him in a car-chase scene, jumping onto the roof of a moving car and running down it. She didn't worry about him. He was well trained and agile as a cat. Then she heard him say, "If you can't find any work with the airlines, maybe you could come out to LA. I could get you some stunt work."

She stiffened. *No.* Park was not cut out for stunt work. He was slow and methodical, not agile and quick. Besides, she'd just got him back in Connecticut. He couldn't just up and leave so soon.

"Maybe," Park said. "I'll let you know."

"It's fun," Ty said. "And it pays well."

She turned. "He doesn't know how to do stunts."

"I'll train him," Ty said. "Mind your own beeswax. This is a private conversation."

Park stared at her, seeming to notice she was made up for the first time. His gaze tracked from her eyes, down her nose, across her cheek, to her hair, back to her mouth and then her neck. She held her breath. He finally met her eyes again. "You don't look like yourself."

She waited for the compliment.

None came.

Just a slow blink from Park and then he turned back to Ty.

It felt like a fist wrapped around her heart and squeezed. She quickly turned to face front. She took a deep breath, reaching for her calm center. She didn't want to snarl at him. She wanted to—ugh! Clueless man! She wanted to shake him! All this work for a slow blink! She could barely focus on whatever Charlotte was saying about the latest workout technique with a swing even though she normally loved to talk fitness and getting strong. She tugged the hem of her dress down a bit. Okay, wait, he hadn't gotten the full effect of her standing in the dress. The reception was where the magic would happen. She slid her ice-cold fingers under her legs.

The seats filled in, and when the music started, they turned as one to see Hailey walking down the aisle, looking like a beautiful princess, smiling as though she enjoyed being the center of attention. And then came Claire in a stunning gown with a big poufy bottom like they'd all seen in *Gone with the Wind*, a previous book club selection. They'd watched the movie after reading the book. Claire's dad walked her down the aisle. She knew the dress was custom made for Claire by some famous designer. Claire wore a veil over her face, but Mad could still make out her expression, smiling and confident. Jake stared hard, love shining in his eyes. An unexpected lump formed in her throat.

The officiant was local, a judge who'd been paid well to keep the wedding quiet. He led them in the vows and, when Jake said his part of the vow, silent tears leaked out of Claire's eyes. And, for some stupid reason, Mad's too. She sniffled and carefully wiped under her eyes, hoping she hadn't ruined her makeup.

Josh stared at Hailey standing on the other side of Claire. Hailey stared at Jake, a pleasant expression pasted on her face as if she knew there would be pictures.

When Claire said her part of the vows, through tears that Jake brushed away gently with his thumbs, Mad lost it, a small sob escaping before more tears streamed down her face. Geez. She was going to ruin all of Hailey's hard work on her face. It was just the first time she'd been at a wedding with two people she loved, and feeling the love between them at the same time was overwhelming.

A white handkerchief wiggled next to her shoulder.

"Thanks," she said over her shoulder and saw it was from Park.

He pressed his lips together, looking concerned. She knew he didn't like it when she cried. She rarely did. But as a kid when she occasionally lost it, Park was always the one there for her, silently comforting her with a tissue or a sympathetic look. One time he gathered his allowance, a collection of quarters, and bought her a chocolate bar.

She wondered for a moment why Park carried a white handkerchief, figured it probably came with the suit, and wiped carefully under her eyes where she figured there would be smeared mascara. Nothing came off. Hailey smiled at her. She blinked a few times and smiled back. The woman had her back with the waterproof stuff.

She sniffled and held the handkerchief tightly in her hand. Park had always had her back too. How could she not love him?

The ceremony ended to applause as Jake and Claire kissed for the first time as husband and wife. Her friends whooped and whistled. She felt another sob threaten and looked to the ceiling. Tears spilled over her cheeks anyway. A warm hand gripped her shoulder and squeezed briefly. She knew without looking that it was Park. Ty was more likely to clap her on the back.

Claire and Jake ran down the small aisle, hand in hand, beaming.

She stood and watched them go, wiping her tears once more. She met Park's sympathetic eyes. "I'm fine. Thanks for the handkerchief."

"It was from your dad. He gave it to me to give to you."

"Oh."

Her dad had already moved down the aisle away from her.

"Guess I'll thank him, then." She felt like an idiot, reading so much into Park's every move. She had to stop remembering the way he was in the past and try to see him for who he was now. It was only fair if that was what she wanted from him.

Hailey and Josh walked down the aisle together, a sharp contrast of Hailey's sunny bright looks and Josh's serious dark looks. Josh escorted her in a gentlemanly way, offering his arm. Their dad had drilled gentlemanly manners into all of her brothers. It took for some better than others. Hailey looked like she was walking in front of the judges at a beauty pageant, poised and controlled, a smile plastered on her face.

They all reconvened in the formal living room, where round tables held glasses of champagne for everyone. They toasted and drank champagne for a cocktail hour while they waited for the limos that would take them to the reception.

Hailey appeared at her side. "I saw you crying at the wedding, you softie."

Mad adjusted the lace shawl more firmly around her. "It was Claire. The minute she started crying, I started crying. It's contagious."

"Lauren and Carrie were crying too," Hailey said.

Mad glanced over at them, happy and drinking champagne now. "I feel a little better."

"Park helped you out, though," Hailey said with a smile.

"It was a handkerchief from my dad," Mad said. "He was just the messenger."

"Don't you worry," Hailey said in a voice of steel. "The night is young. I haven't failed yet in my efforts." She narrowed her eyes. "Who am I?"

Mad rolled her eyes and droned, "The love junkie." It was on her professional wedding planner business card.

"And what do I do?"

"Make love bloom," Mad mumbled, glad Park was on the far side of the room with Ty.

"Correct!"

Mad snagged a flute of champagne and sipped, her gaze traveling back to Park. He held a full glass of champagne and didn't sip. He might have the occasional beer with the guys, but he was rarely drunk. Except for the night he left. What would've happened if he hadn't been drunk that night? Would her life have been different if she'd had the chance to be with him? To express how she really felt about him? Would his life have been different? Probably not. He still would've been locked in to Air Force duty.

He caught her eye across the room and turned away.

"He keeps sneaking peeks at you," Hailey said.

"He's not," Mad said. "He's only looking at me because I'm looking at him."

"What do you think, Char?" Hailey called, pulling Charlotte closer within earshot.

Charlotte's brown eyes sparkled in anticipation of something fun with Hailey. "Huh? Think about what?"

"Is Park looking over at this hot thing?" Hailey said, tilting her head toward Mad.

Mad snorted and fought back the blush.

Charlotte made a big gesture of looking around the entire room before reporting back, tilting her head to make her long brown hair partially cover her face. "Yup."

"What!" Mad exclaimed, her gaze darting back to Park. He was looking at Ty. "Stop messing with me. He is not."

Charlotte smoothed her hair back from her face. "Just go over there."

Mad was not prepared to make a move with Ty as witness.

Hailey put a stop to that line of thinking. "No. We have to separate him from the herd. She can't flirt with her brothers as witnesses. Especially Ty. He'll put her in a headlock or something. Geez. Your brothers are forever messing up your hair. Tell them to knock it off. It took hours to get this look."

"No kidding," Mad said. "You think they care?"

"We need a helmet around you with spikes," Charlotte said.

"Yes, that's attractive," Hailey said with a rare sarcasm that had them cracking up.

"Happy Endings Book Club party," a chauffer called.

"That's us!" Hailey caroled, gesturing for them to follow.

They piled into the limo, where they passed around another bottle of champagne conveniently provided by Claire, not bothering with the plastic glasses. Mad took in her friends—Hailey, Charlotte, Lauren, Carrie, and Ally—and found herself smiling goofily.

"Okay," Mad announced after taking a nice long swig of champagne. "You heard it here first. I'm heading out on the dance floor for a slow dance with Park. Step one in seduction."

The women cheered.

Mad laughed and then hiccupped. "I need all of you out there with me so I don't stick out. I've never danced before."

"What do you mean you've never danced before?" Charlotte asked from across the limo. "Never? Not even at prom?"

"I went as Darth Vader to the prom," Mad said solemnly.

The women stared and then burst out laughing.

"I remember you said that once," Hailey said, taking the champagne bottle from Mad. "But you took the costume off at some point, right?"

Mad snorted. "Are you kidding? The guys loved it. We were all having light saber battles."

"I'll bet the girls loved having their dates hanging out with Darth Vader instead of them," Charlotte said drily.

Mad had never thought about that. She'd just felt like a loser because no one asked her to the prom, so she went by herself in the only way that would make her feel comfortable—covered head to toe in black.

"Anyway," Mad said, "no one wanted to ask the dark side to dance."

"Oh, Mad," her friends said in near unison notes

of sympathy.

"I know," Mad said. "Pathetic, right? That's why I need you all around me, kind of circle me so no one notices my dorky moves."

"You will not be dorky," Hailey proclaimed. "You'll simply put your arms around his neck and let him take the lead."

"What if he doesn't?" Mad asked.

Hailey rolled her eyes. "Then you'll just stand there in each other's arms. That's not so bad, is it?"

Mad smiled widely. "That sounds awesome."

"That's step one," Hailey said. "Step two is the flirt and retreat."

"The what?" Mad asked.

"You're going to touch him as much as possible," Hailey said. "His arm, his shoulder, his hand, and ask him questions."

"Won't that be obvious?" Mad asked.

Hailey put her hand on Mad's arm. "What do you mean?" She looked pointedly at her hand on Mad's arm.

"Okay, I get it," Mad said. "Ask lots of dumb questions and touch his arm."

"Not dumb questions," Charlotte said. "Just say stuff."

"Like what?" Mad asked.

Charlotte waved a hand airily. "Like nice wedding.

Great music. Whatever comes to mind."

Hailey nodded. "And then you come back to us and give him some time to miss you. That's the retreat."

Mad went to take the champagne bottle back from Hailey, but she passed it across to Charlotte. Mad blew out a breath. "I had no idea this seduction stuff was so complicated."

"What do you normally do?" Charlotte asked, taking a slug of champagne.

"Honestly?" Mad smirked as the women all leaned in. "I just tell a guy, usually after a softball game or a sparring match, that I'd like to get sweaty between the sheets."

Lauren gasped. Ally and Carrie stared incredulously.

"That'll work," Charlotte said with a shrug.

"What do you do after?" Hailey asked.

Mad lifted one shoulder up and down. "I say thanks, that won't be happening again and leave."

The women stared. Like maybe that was weird or something.

"Park's different though," Mad said. "Special, you know?"

The women nodded solemnly.

Hailey gave her hand a squeeze. "We know. You'll do great." She tapped a pink fingernail against her pink lips. "Now who should all of you dance with?" She took in their friends and Mad just knew she was thinking long-term strategy for all the future matches she wanted to make. Like it or not, here comes love! Or at least a hookup. Mad would take either one at this point. She just had to get Park out of her system so she could stop obsessing over him, and if that led to something more, great. If not, she'd survive, stronger for having the courage to try.

Feeling pleased with her new philosophical outlook, she actually looked forward to the reception.

CHAPTER EIGHT

Park stood with Ty at the open bar at the wedding reception, waiting for a drink, both of their gazes on the group of women talking and laughing across the room, clustered close together the way women did. They were beautiful one and all, but most especially Mad. He couldn't take his eyes off her. Her hair was smooth and soft looking, more like he remembered it from when she was younger. Her face lit up, glowing, and that body. He'd seen her in workout clothes, knew her petite curves, but that dress was something else. Form-fitting, showing her off in all the right places. A lacy black cover-up kept slipping off one smooth shoulder and she kept hitching it back up. It was driving him crazy. He wanted to rip the thing off her. He wanted to span his hands around her tiny waist and slide them over the curve of her hip.

He turned away, gut churning. The Campbells were family. The only real family he'd ever had. He owed his life to Joe Campbell, who'd taken him in, literally, moving Park into his already crowded household. Mr. Campbell offered to foster him, but Park's mom wouldn't sign off on it. She hit rock bottom six months after Park was rescued from the hellhole he called home and finally went into rehab for heroin addiction. When she got out again, she never asked for him back. He didn't want to go back. She'd show up at school or one of his baseball games sometimes just to make sure he was still alive. The visits only sent him into a rage all over again. The feelings of abandonment and shame made him so angry he'd pick a fight with someone, usually someone older and bigger so he could really let loose. Mr. Campbell had put an end to that finally on Park's twelfth birthday.

"You're twelve now; that's a big deal," Mr. Campbell had said, sitting him down on the sofa in the living room after a small Campbell family birthday party that overwhelmed Park. His birthday with his single druggie mom had always been a painful reminder to her that she was getting older and nothing special for him. Mr. Campbell had sent the others outside, though Park suspected Mad was hiding somewhere eavesdropping. The nine-year-old twerp was forever hanging around the big kids.

Park sat up straighter on the sofa. "Yes, sir."

Mr. Campbell leaned forward, elbows on his knees, from where he sat in his recliner chair. "This is a critical time for you to choose the path your life is gonna take. Are you gonna be a man who uses his fists when he can't handle life or be a man who thinks first and takes action that will set him on a good path?"

Park didn't reply. It was an obvious answer with a not-so-easy solution.

Mr. Campbell went on. "I don't like all the fights you're getting in. This is a destructive pattern, and I want it to stop." His kind brown eyes met Park's. "But you have to want that too."

Park swallowed hard. He never wanted to disappoint Mr. Campbell. He always felt like he had to tread carefully in case Mr. Campbell changed his mind about him. "Yes, sir. I'll try to do better."

Mr. Campbell studied him for a long moment, taking his measure as a man, Park supposed. Park squared his shoulders, trying to be that man.

The older man spoke quietly. "You need to forgive your mom. She is what she is and you can't change that. This is your family now. And I'm not just talking Campbells. I'm talking Ethan, Zach, Marcus, Ben, Nick. All of us are your family." Those were the guys they hung around with from the Police Athletic League. They were over at the house all the time.

Park nodded.

"Your mom will always be a part of you, but she doesn't have to be everything. She doesn't have to rule you."

"Yeah!" a pip-squeak voice chimed in. They both turned to see Mad peeking through the railing at the top of the stairs, where she must've been listening. Her dark brown hair was in a crooked ponytail, her brown eyes large in her face like a baby deer. Innocent. Fragile. "Your mom sucks!"

Honest.

"Madison Campbell," Mr. Campbell barked, "we'll be having a talk as soon as I'm done here with Park."

Mad stood, leaning over the railing from the top of the stairs, making Park's heart pound hard. It was nearly a ten-foot drop. He had to keep her alive.

"Get off the railing!" Park hollered.

She leaned even further over, grinning with a big gap of missing front teeth. Fearless as ever. "My mom sucks too. Don't worry, Park, you got us." Her *s*'s lisped from the gap in her teeth, reminding him how little she was. She raised a small clenched fist in solidarity.

He raised a fist back.

She hitched one denim-clad leg over the railing, and his heart stopped and then lurched painfully on as she slid down the railing in a blur. She crossed to him and made their fists bump.

"Go outside with your brothers," Mr. Campbell snapped. "You're in trouble, young lady."

Mad strolled toward the front door, all sass and attitude.

"Coat," Mr. Campbell ordered.

Mad snagged her red coat off the hook in the hall closet and carried it outside, not bothering to put it on even though it was February. Before the door shut behind her, they heard her holler to her brothers, "Dad says you have to let me play."

Park fought back a grin. Her brothers hated having her on their team for anything because she was little and slow (compared to them). Park was the one who made sure she was included. He knew it sucked to feel like you were all alone, watching everyone else have fun.

Mr. Campbell took a deep breath and turned back to Park. "Do you understand what I'm trying to say? I want you to dig deep for that inner strength I know is in there and choose a different path. No more fistfights."

"Yes, sir." He wanted to be strong like Mr. Campbell. His own dad was weak, an alcoholic who split when Park's baby sister died.

Mr. Campbell smiled, laugh lines forming around his eyes. "When're you going to call me Dad? You've lived here two years. I told you you're one of us."

"Yes, sir, Dad."

Mr. Campbell, his honorary dad, stood, held out a hand and pulled Park to his feet. His dad hugged him in a big bear hug. Park could count on one hand the number of times he'd been hugged. He felt surrounded by strength and love. Most of his previous hugs had been the quick kind from the very physical older brother Ty Campbell hugging him and pounding him on the back for scoring a goal or a basket. This felt different. Important.

His dad pulled back and ruffled Park's hair. "All right, go outside and shoot hoops with the guys while I have a talk with Miss Sassy Pants."

"Lotta beauties at this party," Ty commented, jolting Park out of his memories.

"I guess," Park muttered.

"Weddings are a great place for a pickup," Ty said. "They're feeling all romantic and lonely. Then you just swoop in."

Park snorted. "Yeah? Which one you think you're gonna just swoop in on?"

"I like the looks of the one in the yellow dress."

Park shifted, surreptitiously checking her out under half-hooded eyes. "She's all right."

"All right? You need to get your eyes checked. I think she's a personal trainer. Or maybe she just has a personal trainer. Who cares? Look at those legs."

"Look at her face," Park said. "That face says I don't tolerate fools."

Ty socked his shoulder. "Watch and learn, my friend."

Their drinks arrived, two ice-cold beers, and they wandered over to where his brothers were congratulating Jake and Claire, who'd just arrived after pictures. Hailey stepped away from the pack and headed for her book club posse.

"Hailey," Ty called.

She stopped and turned on her heel. "Yes?"

"Who's the girl in the yellow dress?"

She glanced over at her friends and then headed over to Ty. "Charlotte. You want me to introduce you?"

Ty's eyes traveled over Charlotte again from head to toe. "Nah. Just curious."

She cocked her head. "Sure?"

"Not everyone appreciates a matchmaking wedding planner, princess," Josh drawled, appearing at Hailey's side. He gave her a devious smile like he couldn't wait to mess with her.

Hailey huffed. "I am a happy ending facilitator. This wedding is proof!"

Josh leered. "Well, now, I don't have *any* problem with a happy ending."

Hailey flushed bright pink. "It's not that kind of happy ending."

Josh leaned close, but they could still hear him loud and clear. "Maybe it should be. Maybe you'd have more men interested in your singles book club instead of all those women."

Hailey's hand fluttered in the air. "I have no problem getting a man interested."

Josh barked out a laugh. Ty and Park exchanged an amused look. These two were a riot.

"Su-u-re," Josh said with a slow nod. "That's why you had to pay me for wedding dates."

Hailey threw her hands up. "That was business! Not a date!"

Josh smirked.

"Shut up!" Hailey stalked away.

Ty shoved Josh by the shoulder. "Why don't you just hook up and get it over with?"

"Fuck you," Josh said casually, his gaze following Hailey's curvy ass.

"She paid for wedding dates?" Park asked. He couldn't imagine why. The woman was the kind of beautiful that you normally only saw in the movies or on TV.

"Yup," Ty said. "Paid Joshy here as part of her business plan. That ended well, as you can see."

Park shook his head. Josh grinned.

Their dad came over, the hard lines in his face easily breaking into a smile. "It was a beautiful wedding, wasn't it?"

His dad, despite being single for so many years, was still a bit of a romantic. His wife had left when Mad was only one, yet he still spoke of her fondly. He even kept their wedding picture on the bedroom wall. It kept him stuck, Park thought. But his dad seemed content, happy being a dad to so many, so they never spoke of it.

"Yeah," Ty said. "Jake's a lucky bastard. Coulda been Josh if they hadn't pulled a twin switcheroo on that blind date."

Josh shook his head. "Nah. Claire got the right twin. I would hate having all those reporters nosing around and the paparazzi with their cameras." He shuddered.

"I didn't see any at the wedding," Park said.

"That's because Claire kept everything secret and it's just a small group," his dad said. "Her bodyguard arranged security for the reception. They're posted outside of the room and around the resort. Even if they do have a leak somewhere, it'll be contained."

Park could see how that would get old. Always feeling like you were being watched.

A short while later, they all went to the round tables for a sit-down meal. The book club women sat together. The brothers sat at another table, with some of them also sitting with Claire's family and some of Jake's friends. It was a pretty large room for such a small party, but the view was spectacular. The ballroom was on a cliff with floor-to-ceiling windows overlooking the Atlantic Ocean.

After the meal of filet mignon and lobster, a live band played a slow ballad and the newlyweds were called onto the dance floor.

Park watched Claire and Jake looking so happy and in love. Their bodies pressed close, their gazes locked. It was the first time Park had been at a wedding of someone close to him and, just like at the ceremony, his chest ached. He knew it wasn't just him. Even Mad had gotten weepy at the ceremony. He would've hugged her if they'd been in the same row. It pained him to watch her cry without offering comfort. He'd done what he could.

The band leader spoke into the mike with a deep smooth voice. "Next dance is for the wedding party."

Jake and Claire went to the head table to watch. Josh crooked his finger at Hailey, and she strode over to him, head held high. Josh offered his arm and she took it, walking with him to the center of the dance floor. Once there, Josh took her hand, the other resting on her back, leaving plenty of space between them as he led them in a slow waltz. He didn't know

Josh knew how to dance like that. The pair practically glided around the dance floor, seeming surprisingly in synch for all the hostility between them.

"Ask Charlotte to dance on the next one," Ty told Park.

Park cocked his head. "Why? I thought you wanted her."

"I do. I'm going to ask Hailey."

"What? Why?"

"Just do it."

"I don't want to dance."

"You have to," Ty said. "There's a ton of women here. You gotta do your part."

"There's other guys here," he said, gesturing around the table. "There's more guys than girls anyway."

"I thought you'd be my wingman," Ty said.

"Get Alex." Ty and Alex had spent a lot of time together as teens picking up girls.

"He's too busy with Viv."

Park glanced over to where Alex was carrying a crying Viv out of the ballroom.

"She's tired," Ty said by way of explanation. "She missed her afternoon nap."

"Is he coming back?"

"Probably. He'll carry her around a bit and, after she falls asleep, he'll bring her back. She'll probably sleep through the noise. She's used to it."

"No babysitter?"

Ty shifted to watch Charlotte. "Babysitter quit when Viv proved to be too much of a handful. She's fine. Plenty of family around to help out."

But Park didn't see anyone helping out. Just Alex on his own.

When the next song started, everyone was invited to join the wedding party. One by one, his brothers stood, going to ask a woman to dance. Park stayed put and pulled out his cell phone to take some pictures.

Someone tapped him on the shoulder. He turned, his heart thumping a little harder at the sight of Mad up close in that tight black dress. The black lace cover-up shifted off one shoulder, exposing smooth skin. His gaze drifted over her shoulder to her delicate collarbone, and then lower to the soft swell of—he stopped and swallowed. The dark line of a tattoo peeked out of the dress right over her heart. He wanted to trace it, wanted to see all of it.

"Hey, PMS," she said. Her old nickname for him when he got moody and broody.

"You got a tattoo," he said, unable to take his eyes off it.

She peeked down and hiked up the front of her dress to cover it. Then she adjusted the lacy cover-up over both her shoulders. He wanted to peel that lacy thing off her, desperately wanted to peel that dress down. He needed to see—

"You just gonna sit here all night?" she demanded.

He stood automatically, in a weird place between shocked at her stunning beauty and wary. Like a distant siren call of danger was trying to get through his hazy brain. Seeing her across the room was one thing. Up close and personal, something else entirely. She smelled like flowers. Mad never smelled like flowers.

"Take a picture, it lasts longer," she snapped.

He aimed his cell at her and did exactly that. She looked a little pouty. He brushed his thumb across her full lower lip before he realized what he was doing. The roar of his heartbeat pounded in his ears. He pressed his thumb against it, right in the center. So soft. Her lips parted.

His voice came out husky. "You look so different."

Her deep brown eyes went soft.

He dropped his hand.

"Thanks," she said softly before taking off the lace cover-up and draping it over the back of his chair. Her curvy little body in a tight black dress, exposed to his eyes and hands, made everything in him stand at full attention. The siren call of danger rang loud and clear in his mind. She was too close.

He elbowed her, making a little space between

them. "What the hell did those women do to you?" He figured her friends had something to do with her new look. He'd never seen her like this, all made-up and sexy. Thankfully.

Her eyes flashed hurt. "Excuse me for wearing a dress to a wedding."

He hadn't meant to hurt her feelings. He was just bowled over at the change in her.

She crossed her arms, making her cleavage lift. He risked another look at her tattoo, but couldn't see it. He forced his gaze back to her face.

Her lip curled belligerently. "Since we're both dressed up, we should dance or something."

"I can't dance," he said, but what he meant was *I can't dance with you*. He couldn't hold her close, couldn't have those petite curves pressed against him. The fact that she was the off-limits Campbell girl was rapidly fading in his mind as everything in him urged him to touch, to taste, to claim. His heart pounded out the message *danger, danger, danger*.

"Like I give a shit," she said, grabbing his hand and yanking him toward the dance floor. "I'm not dancing with my brothers."

"Ask Claire's brother," he said lamely, digging his heels in on the edge of the dance floor.

"You're dumber than you look," she said, putting her arms around his neck and pressing close.

His hands automatically went to her narrow waist, spanning his fingers wide to touch more of her. The room dimmed around them, the music distant, nothing but the sweet scent of flowers, the heat of her, his head swimming in a strange cocktail of lust and danger.

She swayed against him, and he realized he should be moving. He swayed back and forth a bit with her, and she somehow managed to settle in even closer to him. There was no part of him that wasn't aware of her. Her breasts pressed into his chest, her belly against his aching groin, her upper thighs against his. His hand found the satiny skin of her bare back.

"Hey, shortstack," Ty said from nearby where he was dancing with Hailey.

"Hi, guys!" Hailey said with a big smile.

Park lifted his chin in acknowledgment and tried to put some space between him and Mad, but Mad had a good hold on him and it was impossible.

"Hi," Mad said, shifting them away from Ty and Hailey.

Park tried not to focus on Mad in his arms. He craned his neck, looking around for the girl in the yellow dress. She was dancing with Ethan. *Great plan, Ty.* Ethan was smooth with women and could easily move in on her.

Mad went up on tiptoe, brushing against him and

gaining his undivided attention. Then she whispered in his ear, her voice a sexy purr, "You look hot in that suit."

He swallowed hard because he now knew without a doubt the attraction went both ways. She'd desired him once, when she was too young, and he'd hoped that when he returned, she'd have moved on. He was damaged goods.

"Thanks," he managed.

She brushed against him a second time as she stood flat on her feet again. His cock throbbed with need, his brain screaming at him to pull away. *Danger. Off-limits. Not her.*

She met his eyes, a small smile playing over her lips like maybe she'd noticed the effect she had on him. "It was like the beauty shop of horror with my friends before the wedding."

"Horror?"

"You don't want to know what women do behind closed doors." Her breasts brushed across his chest as she swayed right to his sway left. Was she wearing a bra? *Don't look.*

She went on. "But hopefully it's all worth it." She swayed left to his sway right, brushing her breasts against him again. He took the lead, a hand on her lower back, making sure she swayed *with* him to prevent any further brushing. "With pain comes beauty, least that's what Hailey says. I'm not sure I buy it."

He met her eyes, wanting to tell her how beautiful she looked. How jaw-dropping sexy. But it was Mad. His little pip-squeak to protect at all costs. Even if that meant protecting her from himself.

She sure as hell didn't feel like a little pip-squeak right now.

She felt hot and sweet and right in his arms. She could never be his, he reminded himself. She deserved so much more than he could give. He just wasn't made that way.

"You don't have to say it," she said like she could read his freaking mind.

"Say what?" he asked cautiously.

She gave him a smirky knowing look. "You dig the dress." She clearly felt the proof during their dance and he saw no reason to deny it now.

He leaned down to her ear and whispered, "I nearly swallowed my tongue when I saw you."

She pulled back to look at him, eyes wide.

He returned her gaze, letting her see it was true, yet knowing it had to end right here on the dance floor. He didn't know how much time passed, the two of them just standing there, staring at each other. He suddenly realized people were leaving the dance floor. The song had ended.

He pulled away. "Thanks for the dance, little bit."

And then he turned and walked straight out the door, through the hotel's long lobby and outside, desperately needing to cool off in the winter air.

CHAPTER NINE

Mad strode as quickly as she could in her clunky heels over to her friends the moment Park left her standing on the dance floor like an idiot.

Hailey elbowed her. "So, how'd it go?"

"He practically ran away from me the moment the song ended," Mad said with a scowl.

"He was holding you pretty close," Hailey said.

"No, he wasn't," Mad said. "That was me pressing against him."

"Did he say anything at all complimentary about your new look?" Charlotte asked.

The women leaned in, eager for the details.

Mad sighed. "He did say he about swallowed his tongue when he saw me."

The women exclaimed excitedly over this news. "That's great!" Ally chirped.

"A very good sign," Carrie said.

"Get back in there, tiger," Hailey said.

"He left," Mad said.

"He'll be back," Charlotte said. "It's early."

"Just keep it up and be nice," Hailey said. "And for heaven's sake, stop curling your lip."

"Nice, nice, nice," Mad muttered. "Maybe we should send Lauren over there."

"Where is Lauren?" Hailey asked, looking around. "Aww, she's holding your niece."

Mad looked over to where Lauren was sitting in a chair with Viv curled in her lap, sound asleep, her head leaning against Lauren's shoulder. She wondered where Alex was.

"Which one of your brothers is a good dancer?" Charlotte asked. "I love to dance."

"Slow or fast?" Mad asked.

"Fast."

"None of them."

"Slow."

"Probably Jake or Josh. They won't step on your toes."

"Hello, beautiful," Ty crooned, holding his hand out to Ally. "Would you like to dance?"

Ally tittered and took his hand.

Mad stood there with her friends, watching the dance floor. She knew the minute Park returned. He found her dad at the far end of the room, gazing out at the ocean. Her dad turned and clapped a hand on

Park's shoulder. They had a tight bond and she was glad for that, Park needed it. She wouldn't ask him to dance again, she decided. He had to ask her. But he didn't. Instead she stood there as dance after dance, Ty came up and asked each of her friends to dance. Every single one except Charlotte. In fact, he went out of his way to look at Charlotte and then ask someone else to dance. Moron.

Charlotte pointedly ignored Ty, instead focusing on coaching Mad, with Hailey enthusiastically agreeing. "Let's take your flirting to the next level," Charlotte said. "Touch yourself and it'll make him think about touching you."

"Myself?" Mad asked.

Charlotte demonstrated by lifting her breasts, smoothing her hands down her sides, and touching her neck.

"She's right," Hailey said.

"Look up at him too," Charlotte said. "Guys love that."

"I have to look up at him," Mad said. "He's taller." She remembered how Park always favored petite pretty women. They always seemed so delicate and girly. She wasn't sure she could ever be girly enough for him.

"Go now," Hailey urged when she saw Park had moved to sit with Josh.

"No, not now," Mad said. "Josh will ruin it."

"I'll distract Josh," Hailey said, wiggling her fingers at him. Josh ignored her.

"Forget it," Mad said. "I'm not ready. I need another drink."

"No more drinks," Hailey said. "You'll look sloppy drunk."

"I've only had two glasses of champagne," Mad protested. "That's nothing."

"Fine," Hailey said. "I'll get you one glass of wine and that's it." She left.

Ty returned, looked between Mad and Charlotte, and asked Mad to dance. Charlotte bristled at her side.

"Bite me," Mad said. Ty was purposely asking every one of her friends to dance except Charlotte, which meant he probably wanted to dance with Charlotte most of all. Mad refused to play into his ploy.

Ty looked to Charlotte, who crossed the room to ask Josh to dance.

And then Charlotte danced with literally every man in attendance except Ty. She was an amazing dancer, slow or fast. Mad sipped the white wine Hailey had brought her. It was just her and Ty now, watching Charlotte dance, and she wondered if he'd finally step up. Charlotte had this confident way of tossing her long brown hair that really worked (if only Mad had long hair) and a sensuous shimmy that Mad wasn't sure she could get away with.

Finally Charlotte returned to where Ty and Mad were standing. She grabbed her water from a nearby table and took a long drink. Ty looked at her expectantly.

Charlotte smiled at Mad. "Hey, girl, you gotta get out there with me."

"Maybe," Mad said.

"You looked like you were having fun," Ty said with a scowl.

Charlotte's brown eyes narrowed. "I was." She finished her water in one long swallow and set the glass on the table.

"With every guy here," Ty said, "except one."

Charlotte did a head swivel. "And why is that?" She crossed her arms. "Why did you make it a point to ask everyone to dance but me?"

Ty crossed his arms. "I didn't."

"Liar," Mad put in, but they didn't seem to notice her in their standoff.

"So dance with me now," Charlotte said.

Ty barked out a laugh. "You asking me to dance?"

"Oh, so you're playing hard to get." Charlotte nodded sagely. "That's your game."

He grinned. "It worked, didn't it? Here you are asking me to dance."

Charlotte lifted her chin. "I don't play games."

"Yeah, you do, sweetheart." Ty took her hand. "Shall we?"

Charlotte pulled her hand from his grip. "I'm also hard to get." She turned and walked back to Ethan, asking him to dance. He did, pulling her straight into his arms. Charlotte looked over Ethan's shoulder and gave Ty a smug smile.

Ty grumbled to himself. Her brothers were idiots. And Mad was tired of being in their company. She strode over to Park, who was finally done talking to Josh and heading back in her direction. She put a little wiggle into her hips like Charlotte and stopped in front of him, looking up at him as Charlotte instructed.

He eyed her. "Your ankle giving you trouble? You were walking a little funny."

She put a hand on his arm. "My ankle's fine. I can't help it if my hips move when I walk." She put her hands on her waist and slid them down her hips. *Touching myself. So hot.*

His gaze followed her hands and then snapped back to her eyes. "It didn't look like your hip—never mind. What's up?"

"Not much. Just standing around at a wedding, watching other people dance." She swayed a bit in time to the music, her gaze on all the slow-dancing couples. She wouldn't ask him to dance again.

"Mad?"

Score! She turned and gave him a sultry, inviting smile. "Yeah?"

His eyes locked on her chest. She peeked at herself. Still covered. "What kind of tattoo did you get?"

"You want a peek?"

He swallowed visibly.

"You know you want to," she said in a low voice, daring him.

His voice was gruff. "Just tell me what it is."

"I'd rather show you."

"That's not a good idea." But his hot gaze said otherwise.

"Sure it is," she said gamely. Like this was all just fun and games. Like her heart wasn't in her throat.

"Mad," he said gently. He cleared his throat and gazed out at the dance floor. "You're special. I would never treat you like that."

"Treat me like what?"

He met her eyes with a pained look. "You deserve better than me."

"What do you mean?"

He shook his head slowly. "One day you're going to meet some great guy who can give you everything you deserve."

She put a hand on his arm, needing to get through to him. "I know what I want."

His jaw clenched tight. "I don't want to hurt you."

"I won't break," she said quietly.

He stared at her for so long her heart swelled with hope. She could tell he was letting that sink in, considering what it meant. That she could handle him.

Someone clanged on glassware. "Gather around for cutting the cake."

Park inclined his head. "Better get in on the cake before your brothers finish it off."

Mad stood there for a moment, torn between wrenching disappointment and very motivating aggravation. She met his eyes directly. "I'm coming for you, Park."

~ ~ ~

Park stood near the front of the circle gathered around Claire and Jake cutting the wedding cake. Not that he cared about cake. He just needed to get away from the sleek heat of Mad doing her damnedest to entice him. The photographer got in close as Jake and Claire cut into the cake, both of their hands guiding the knife. He tried to focus, but his mind kept tripping back to Mad.

Mad in that slinky black dress pressed against him.

Mad with adoration in her eyes, believing him to be a better man than he ever could be.

Mad coming for him.

That hit him in a double whammy—heart and groin—as his brain translated a very different meaning. It was one thing to deny his own attraction, near hell to deny hers too. The temptation to cross that line battled with his need to keep her from getting hurt.

His gaze drifted across the circle to where Mad stood with her friends. He found it hard not to notice her. He'd spent most of his life making sure she was okay. Even when he was away, he checked in on her, checked in with Josh too, who spent the most time with her. He kept space between them the rest of the night. It was the only way he could think of to keep his hands off her. As soon as the reception ended, he headed back to his room upstairs.

Once safely inside his room, he stripped down to his undershirt and boxer briefs and flopped down on the bed. He turned off the light and threw an arm over his eyes as if that would banish Mad from his mind. Next thing he knew a vision of a younger Mad flooded his brain. The night of his going-away party.

The night she wore his blue flannel shirt with a ripped revealing shirt underneath.

The night he first realized Mad was going to be trouble for him.

Everyone had said their goodbyes and gone to bed. He'd settled on the sofa, tossing and turning, unable to sleep, knowing he was about to leave the only place that had ever felt like home. He was eighteen and it was time to prove himself as a man. To make his dad proud. An hour passed while he stared at the ceiling, and then he heard her soft footsteps padding down the stairs. They had a full house, but she was the only one with soft footsteps. Her brothers and dad were heavy footed.

He closed his eyes, pretending to be sleeping.

"Park," she whispered.

He didn't respond. Not going there. Not noticing her. Not touching her.

She jabbed him. "Park."

He ignored her.

She sat on the sofa next to him and jabbed him in the ribs. "Park, it's Mad. Wake up."

He groaned and shifted, his ribs smarting. She jabbed him again.

His eyes flew open. "What?"

She leaned close. So close. Her familiar sweet scent tinged with something else, something dangerously close to sexy. "I'm going to miss you," she whispered, her lips only millimeters away.

He closed his eyes, shutting out temptation. "Oh, man, the room's spinning. I drank too much."

He felt her shift away.

"How much did you drink?" she asked suspiciously.

He waved his hand around, feigning drunk. He knew what it looked like, even if he rarely indulged. "Eight beers. Me and Ty had one last party. So-o-o wasted."

The light turned on by the end table. He squinted against the glare. She peered into his eyes. "Your eyes don't look drunk."

"I'm feeling it, believe me." He turned off the light and flopped down on his side. "Go to bed, mini."

Her warm fingers stroked his hair, leaving a tingling trail. "Your hair feels different." Her fingers trailed to his neck. "I'm not mini anymore. I'm all grown up."

He knew what she meant. He'd tried not to notice. She was too young and meant for better than him.

He rolled to his back, covering his eyes with his arm. "Let me sleep this off. Seriously. Wa-a-ay too much to drink." He breathed deeply, feigning the sleep of the drunk, hoping she'd move on. Hoping one day she'd forget him and he'd return to find her with a family man. One who could give her everything she deserved.

He shifted, purposely nudging her off the sofa. She must've been standing next to the sofa now because he didn't hear footsteps walking away and he could still breathe her in.

He heard some movement and held his breath,

hoping she was turning away, when soft lips grazed his, jolting him. He didn't move. He was frozen, yet on fire. She did it again, her lips brushing his and then fitting more firmly against him. Carnal heat rushed through him and he reacted instinctively, kissing her back, and then more, needing to taste. His tongue traced the seam of her lips, and the moment she opened for him, his tongue delved inside her hot mouth. His hand came up, about to pull her on top of him when she moaned and he jerked back to reality. He dropped his hand, broke the kiss, and rolled to his side, giving her his back.

"Park," she whispered urgently, "I want you to be my first."

He nearly groaned, honored in her faith in him and wanting what could never be his. Ty would kill him. Her father would banish him from the only family where he ever truly belonged. He fervently wished he'd met her any other way. Or that somehow he'd never been attracted to her.

He could feel her leaning over him. She was only fifteen. He pretended to be sleeping, even as part of him rebelled, angry that he'd never be her first now. She'd find someone else when he was away. Some jerk that didn't deserve her.

A long moment passed and then she stroked his hair. "Come back in one piece, okay?"

Park let out a long breath. He knew he'd done the right thing back then. He'd left her an innocent girl. Whatever she'd done in the intervening years was none of his business. And now he had to admit she was all grown up, no longer an innocent girl, but a full-grown sexy woman. But that still didn't mean she was for him.

He was too restless to sleep. He propped the pillows behind him, turned on the TV, and stared blankly at some old movie as visions of Mad kept crashing through his mind. Mad in a towel. Mad working out in nothing but a bra. Mad in a sexy dress, that tattoo playing peekaboo, enticing him. Not going there, he told himself sternly. Off-limits. And then he'd see her again in his mind, sleek and toned, a body that was strong and feminine, sexy, so sexy. He scrubbed a hand over his face.

There was a knock at the door.

He jackknifed upright in bed. Was it her? She'd said she was coming for him.

Another knock, louder and more urgent.

He strode to the door, flipped on the light, and looked through the peephole. His heart kicked up, even though he knew he had to end this here and now.

He pulled the door open a crack. "Mad," he started and then trailed off in shock as he realized she was standing in nothing but a blue flannel shirt. His shirt. The shirt from his bittersweet memories. She'd kept it all these years.

He suddenly felt like he had a do-over. To change the outcome of that long-ago night the way he wished he could have if the timing had been right.

She pushed the door open and stepped inside, her deep brown eyes never leaving his. He opened his mouth and shut it again as she slowly unbuttoned the shirt, starting at the top. His gaze dropped, riveted to every inch of exposed skin, knowing what she was finally showing him. And then the shirt fell open and he saw it. His heartbeat thundered in his ears, everything around him dimming as his eyes locked on the small hawk tattoo over her heart. A gift that touched him soul deep.

As if in slow motion, he reached out and placed his palm over the tattoo. Her heart pounded furiously under his hand.

The last of his control snapped.

CHAPTER TEN

"Your heart is racing," Park told her, his voice gravelly as he wrapped an arm around her waist and pulled her close.

She couldn't speak; this was the moment she'd been waiting for her whole adult life. Park touching her. Park wanting her.

He traced the tattoo with one finger, staring at it. "What does it mean to you?" His hazel eyes met hers.

Her mouth was dry. She licked her lips, drawing his gaze. "It means be strong, be fierce." *And it means Park stole my heart.*

He placed his palm over her heart again, covering the hawk. "I'm honored." He dropped his forehead to hers. "So honored."

She couldn't speak over the lump in her throat. He took a step back and pulled off his undershirt in that two-handed way guys did, shifting to show her his left bicep with a larger matching hawk tattoo. He'd gotten it when he enlisted. "For me it means think first before taking action. The hawk observes and then swoops in for the kill."

She gave him a small watery smile and finally put it all out there. "It also means Park swooped in and stole my heart."

His fingers flexed, his hands at his sides. "Mad, this—"

She held his face with both hands. "I'm all grown up. I can handle you."

"I know," he said, his voice gruff with emotion. He snagged her wrists, pulling her hands away from his face and back to her sides. "I don't want to hurt you. I'm not cut out for relationships."

She met his eyes unflinchingly. She'd always known she wasn't woman enough for a man like Park. He favored petite girly girls. "Just once," she said. "Nobody has to know."

He released her wrists, his eyes searching hers and then drifting down to her mouth and lower to the hawk over her heart. She waited breathlessly, needing him to make the next move, willing him to touch her. Finally, his large hand cupped the back of her neck, drawing her close, and then his lips met hers just as electric as she remembered. She wrapped her arms around his neck and pressed her entire body against his. She expected a quick hookup, a rush of grabbing hands and then hard thrusts against the wall, like most of her hookups, but Park surprised her. His hand slid up to cup the back of her head, holding her as he kissed her deeply, tenderly, like he was cherishing her. She'd never been kissed like this in her life. He didn't press her up against the wall, didn't even let his hands roam, merely held her, one hand on her head, his other arm wrapped around her waist. It made her head woozy and her limbs heavy. He kissed her like he had all night, on and on and on, until her lips felt swollen, her entire body liquid heat.

His mouth trailed to her jawline to the sensitive spot under her ear. Both his hands spanned her waist, resting lightly, and she let her hands roam across the muscular planes of his back. She needed more of him, more heat, more skin on skin.

His breath ran hot over her ear as he whispered, "God, Mad, I want you more than is decent."

"Be indecent," she urged.

He let out a long breath. "Not with you."

"Yes, I'm used to it."

He dropped his hands to his sides.

"I can handle it." She slid a hand to the waistband of his briefs, intent on pushing him, when he caught her wrist.

His hazel eyes met hers, the conflict in them clear to her—heat and restraint. He pulled her close in a tight hug, his words rasping in her ear like he'd run a long distance. "You'll never look at me the same way again." He released her. "I need you to step away now, turn, run—"

She grabbed his head and kissed him passionately. She never ran from trouble; she invited it. The kiss turned urgent, openly carnal, igniting her. His fingers speared through her hair in a tight grip; his other hand went to the small of her back, pressing her close against his hard body, his delicious heat. There was a tension in him under all that heat that told her he was holding back, going easy on her. Maybe because he knew it was a onetime thing. Maybe because this was the first time she'd always dreamed of. Their first time.

He shifted to her neck, hot kisses raining down the column of her throat all the way to her collarbone, his tongue tracing the dip between her collarbones. She wanted a lot more.

"Nobody has to know," she reminded him, squeezing his ass with both hands. "Do what you want."

He palmed her ass over the long shirt and then his hand slipped under the shirt, meeting bare skin. He pulled back enough to look at her, the intense heat in his eyes promising a lot more if she could only push through his restraint. "You forgot your panties."

"They didn't work with the dress."

"You're not wearing a dress."

She stepped back, unbuttoned the last few buttons of her shirt, and let it drop to the ground. Park just stood there, taking her in. She hoped he wasn't judging her to be too boyish. Everything about her was small and her hips were narrow. Not super curvy the way men seemed to like.

She got huffy when he kept looking and not touching. "I know I'm too small."

"You're perfect," he said, his arms wrapping around her. He kissed her for a long hot moment and then he pulled back, frustrating her to no end, before placing one large hand over her heart. Everything in her stilled.

He met her eyes, full of heat and tenderness. She swallowed hard, unused to so much emotion with sex. He spoke and the words sounded like a solemn oath. "I'll make it good for you."

Her heart thumped hard and for once she had no smart remark. She could do nothing but stand there and stare. He cupped her jaw, slowly leaning down to kiss her. She fell into it like a soft sigh, a dizzying tumble into deep kisses that turned her to utter mush. He went slow, savoring her, it seemed. He dropped to his knees and cupped one breast, flicking his tongue across the beaded nipple. She arched, aching for more, and he sucked deep. She moaned, desire spearing through her, making her weak with need.

"Park," she whispered, her fingers stroking the soft hair at the nape of his neck.

He gave the other breast the same attention, and she desperately wanted more. His mouth trailed down her belly and dropped a kiss over her sex. She hissed out a breath. His hands cupped her ass as he kissed her intimately, his tongue parting her. She nearly lost it right there. It was so...hot. His dark head, his hot mouth, his hands firm on her. Within minutes she was rocking against him, pleasure flooding her, turning her into a mindless throbbing aching bundle of need. She panted, her fingers tangling in his hair, and then she cried out, tumbling over the edge, the release shaking her up. She dropped her head back, her eyes drifting closed.

He stood and lifted her by the waist. "C'mere, sweet thing."

She wrapped her arms and legs around him and nipped his neck. "I'm not sweet."

"You taste sweet. Let me get another taste to be sure." She throbbed at the words.

He set her on the bed, pushed her legs open, and took another long taste. She writhed under him. "Fuck me," she said on a moan.

He lapped at her again and her hips came off the mattress. "So sweet."

"Okay, I'm sweet. Now fuck me."

He chuckled and buried his face between her legs. She cried out, wiggled this way and that, which only brought him in closer, and then he pushed her legs over his shoulders, keeping her open to him. The pleasure was dark, intense, white-hot. The climax hit suddenly, a deep sensation radiating out from her core as wave after wave of pleasure crashed over her.

She threw her arms to her sides in complete abandon, melting into the mattress. She knew he'd be good. He'd always been so good to her. She heard him shifting away and opened her eyes to find him standing naked next to the nightstand, pulling a condom from his wallet. It was the first time she'd seen him completely naked and he was magnificent. Like a sculpture, all hard lines and planes, defined muscles from his wide shoulders to chest and flat stomach. And, best of all, a thick cock.

"Damn, you're hung," she said appreciatively.

"Thanks." He ripped the foil packet open, knocking his wallet off the nightstand in his haste.

"Guess I shoulda brought a box of condoms for the next round."

"Just once," he said, joining her on the bed.

She ignored the ache in her heart at her own words coming back to her. It didn't matter. She'd sooner die than not have him.

He settled between her legs, holding himself up on his forearms and gazing down at her as he slid slowly inside, filling her. Her breath shuddered out. He kissed her and stroked her hair back from her face. "You okay?"

"I told you I won't break." She lifted her hips, and he groaned. "Make it good."

He thrust again, a slow deep glide. "Haven't I made it good for you so far?"

"It was okay," she said, goading him on. "But I know you're going easy on me—" she flashed a smile "—and I want you to go *hard*."

His eyes glittered, meeting hers for one electrifying moment. He lowered his head, brushing his lips over hers. "You have a sassy mouth," he said and then sank his teeth into her bottom lip.

She scratched her nails down his back and was rewarded with a hard thrust. She wrapped her legs higher around him, taking him deeper. His fingers tangled in her hair as he sucked on the side of her neck and continued a slow in and out.

"Harder, faster," she urged.

"Slower, deeper," he said in a strained voice, doing exactly that. He slid a hand under her ass and held her in place for his insanely slow grind of pleasure.

He gazed into her eyes, and she was caught, drowning in all she felt for him. She was open, too open, and she couldn't survive the inevitable cold shoulder. The brusque goodbye.

She grabbed his ass and pulled him hard against her.

And then she clung to him as his control finally snapped and he pounded into her, taking, taking, taking, his breath harsh and hot near her ear. She tried to memorize everything about this moment, the deep pressure in her core, the heat and strength of him, his scent, and then she lost it, tumbling into the deepest of pleasures, the release shuddering through her, cries of ecstasy wrenched from her throat. His own throaty moan sent him into her with one last deep thrust. Another spark of pleasure shot through her, taking her breath. And then he stilled, their bodies slick with sweat.

He collapsed on top of her. She couldn't have moved anyway. She was so deeply satisfied, limp and boneless.

A long moment later, he rolled off her and padded to the bathroom, probably to get rid of the condom. By the time he returned, she summoned her last reserve of energy and sat up. She had to go before he asked her to leave. She scooted to the edge of the bed and stopped, staring in shock where his wallet had fallen open on the floor. There was a plastic holder for pictures. And the picture right on top was of her.

It was the night of his going-away party. She recognized the ripped concert shirt and his flannel shirt, her long hair in a high ponytail, but what she saw most of all was the love shining in her eyes. He must've known all this time how she worshipped him. She went to pick it up with shaking hands when Park grabbed her and pulled her back against him.

"Stay the night," he said, stroking her hair back. He tucked her more firmly against him, spooning her from behind. "You cold? You're trembling."

She couldn't help it, she was so shocked that he'd carried her picture around all these years.

He settled the covers over her, his arm banding around her waist, his legs tucking against hers. Her throat was clogged with emotion. She debated mentioning the picture. What did it mean? She wanted to look through his wallet, see if there were other pictures. Maybe he had tons of pictures tucked in there. Maybe it was just a coincidence that she was the first picture.

She waited for long moments, until his hold on her loosened, before slowly shifting toward the edge of the bed, intent on snagging the wallet.

Park pulled her back, tucking her against him, his large hand on her head pinning her in place. "Go to sleep, little bit."

"Don't call me that anymore," she said sleepily, the

firm hold and the heat of his body relaxing her. Little bit was a kid nickname and that wasn't where they were at.

He brushed her hair back and kissed her temple. "Go to sleep, sassy mouth."

She bristled, but then he stroked her hair, lulling her. His arm wrapped around her waist again, heavy and secure. She felt so good she finally gave up the fight, closed her eyes, and dropped into a deep sleep.

~ ~ ~

Park woke from a deeply satisfying sleep a little disoriented. He opened his eyes, trying to get his bearings. Hotel. Wedding. He bolted upright. Mad.

She sat on the edge of the bed, going through his wallet.

"What're you doing?" he barked.

She jumped, her cheeks flushing pink. "I was looking at your pictures."

"Who said you could go through my wallet?"

"It was on the floor," she said. "I picked it up. Park, what does this mean?" She held it open, showing him the picture he'd tucked in there. It was from the night he'd left. He'd taken it on his cell phone and, the first chance he got, he had it printed into a picture. That picture had seen him through many a lonely night overseas.

He snagged the wallet and closed it. "Nothing." He leaned over and set it on the nightstand. Next thing he knew Mad was in his lap. Her petite body naked and hot against him. He went instantly hard. Fuck. He didn't have any more condoms and this was supposed to be a onetime thing anyway. He tried to peel her off, but she clung tighter. She was strong too, her cheek pressed against his chest. He was sure she could hear the thundering of his heart.

She looked up at him, her doe-brown eyes searching his. He had her delicate features memorized—the curve of her cheek, her small upturned nose, her pointy chin. "Why do you have my picture in your wallet?"

He blinked, not wanting to hurt her, but at the same time needing her to understand there were boundaries between them, set for her own good.

Her hands roamed on his back, her hot mouth pressed against the side of his neck. He grabbed her by the hair and kissed her hard, unable to resist. She returned the kiss, pressing close, pelvis to pelvis. His instinct to lift her, to sink into oblivion was overwhelming. His fingers tightened in her hair, his other hand on her hip, gripping tight as he fought instinct. But then she grabbed his shoulders, lifting herself, and he had to hold her by the hips with both hands to stop her from sinking down onto him.

"Mad, this was a mistake." How was he going to face his family? How could he face her and see the disappointment in her eyes that he could never be the kind of man she needed?

"Fuck you, this was a mistake," she snapped, her nails digging into his shoulders.

Dark desire thrummed through him. Rough and raw. Not what she deserved.

He closed his eyes. "It was."

She moved quickly, her teeth sinking into his earlobe, giving a sharp tug. He felt himself grow harder, thicker, the need pushing the limits of his control. Her words skimmed hot near his ear. "Open your eyes and see who you're about to fuck."

He opened his eyes to find her glaring at him, the expression on her face defiant, challenging, and strong all at the same time.

He couldn't help himself. He stroked his thumb across her full lower lip and, when her lips parted, pushed inside. Her tongue swirled around his thumb, and he watched as she sucked. He trailed his fingers lower, over her sharp chin, which she lifted, exposing her throat to his rough stroke.

He felt her swallow under his fingers, and he dropped his hand.

They stared at each other for a long moment, his body urging him to take what she offered, his brain slamming on the brakes. The musky scent of arousal made him grip her hips tightly, unsure if he was about to impale her or set her safely away.

Her soft voice reached through the haze of his mind. "I want to know why you have one picture in your wallet and that one picture is of me."

He loosened his grip on her hips, struggling for the words that would be close to the truth without revealing too much. Finally, he said, "Looking at your picture reminded me I had people back home who loved me."

"This wasn't people," she said, rising to her knees and gazing deep into his eyes, mesmerizing him. "This was just—" she suddenly shifted down, taking him fully inside her. He sucked in a harsh breath at the rush of pleasure "—me."

"Mad," he said on a moan. He held her by the hips, knowing he should set her away from him, yet knowing it was way too late for that.

She lifted herself and dropped down on him, taking him deep. His eyes rolled back in his head. She kept going, talking to him as she lifted and dropped over and over, making him crazed, barely hanging onto control.

"Why?" she said on a breathy pant. Another deep slide home. She kept going, kept talking, and he just hung on.

"Why me?" *Tight velvet.*

"*My* picture." *Perfect.*

"*Just* me."

Always you. The voice from deep inside his consciousness made everything in him still.

She moved faster, his mind clouding, sensation and the tight bond he'd always felt with her overwhelming him. He took control, slowing her down before he went off inside her.

"You on the pill?" he asked.

She grinned, like she'd won. "Yes. I want to feel you come inside me. I want all of you."

The words triggered something deep inside, a primal need for possession, and he went for it. Heart-racing exhilaration pumped through his veins as he thrust and she matched him. Everything narrowed down to her, the feel of her petite body clenching around him, her breathy pants, her nails digging into his shoulders. He gripped her sweet ass, and then he went off, holding her tight against him as he emptied himself inside her like he'd never done with another woman before. His woman.

They stayed like that for a long moment, her small frame plastered against him.

She ran her fingers through the hair at the nape of his neck and spoke in his ear. "I know why you had my picture in your wallet."

He pulled back to look at her, all sexily rumpled. And happy. He loved seeing her happy. "Yeah? Why?" This should be good.

"Because you knew I worshipped you."

He couldn't deny he loved the way she looked at him. "Maybe," he allowed.

"Well, guess what?" She lifted off him and slipped out of bed. The loss of her heat, her closeness, made him suddenly bereft.

"What?"

She turned and smiled impishly over her shoulder. "Now it's your turn to worship me."

And with that she went into the bathroom, leaving the door wide open. An invitation.

The shower turned on.

He rolled out of bed. It was his turn.

CHAPTER ELEVEN

The Christmas festivities didn't start until nearly noon. Everyone was sleeping off the long night they'd had of partying at Claire and Jake's wedding reception. Mad showed up at Claire's cabin with Hailey mid-morning, both of them bright-eyed and cheerful. Mad because she'd finally gotten laid by the man of her dreams and Hailey because she was always perky in the morning. Park had left her this morning after their shower, saying he promised to meet up with Ty and Alex to wrap some Santa presents for Viv while she was on a sleigh ride with her grandfather and Claire's parents. Viv was nearly two and understood more this year about Santa.

As was tradition, they had a Secret Santa where they'd all picked a name from the Campbell family, blood brothers included, twenty-dollar max. There were just too many of them for it to be affordable to get everyone a cool gift. She'd drawn Josh this year, which was easy. She'd gotten him an immersion hand mixer for stuff that was too small for the big mixer. It was more than twenty bucks, but, hell, she owed him for everything he'd sacrificed for her. She'd just say she got it on a Black Friday sale.

Claire's cook was preparing a full brunch with waffles, eggs, sausage, bacon, mimosas, fruit salad, and a bagel spread. Mad was on her second cup of coffee in the great room, the cabin filling up with family, while she waited anxiously for Park to arrive. Would he acknowledge her in front of the family? They'd crossed the threshold of just a onetime thing as far as she was concerned. Three times—twice in bed, once in the shower—told her she'd pushed past any resistance he'd had to the two of them. Just a look across the room would satisfy her. Or would he pretend she was nothing more than that mouthy twerp she'd always been to him?

The newlyweds, Jake and Claire, walked downstairs hand in hand, all lovey-dovey smiles. Tomorrow they'd be heading to a honeymoon in the Swiss Alps for a ski vacation. Most of the rest of them were driving home tomorrow. A few of the guys were sticking around to extend their all-expenses-paid vacation.

"There's Mr. Claire Jordan," Mad called to Jake. "How's it feel?"

"Awesome," Jake said, lifting Claire's hand and kissing her palm. Claire beamed.

Claire headed to where Mad and Hailey stood, Jake in tow. "You missed the conga line. Our very last dance went from conga into a crazy bunny hop at the end."

"Thanks to Viv," Jake said with a laugh. "She woke up and wanted in on the action."

"Mad had her own conga going on," Hailey said, bumping her hip.

Mad felt herself flush. She wasn't sure where she stood with Park and didn't want to out them until she knew how he felt about last night. Would he stick to the onetime thing she'd blurted out in her desperation to finally have him?

A man in a bow tie and tweed jacket announced the food was ready. Saved by the bacon! "Let's eat," Mad said, heading to the dining room.

"With who?" Claire asked the minute they arrived at the dining room table. She leaned close for the scoop. "Was it PMS?" Claire had heard about her joking nickname for Park at the reception last night. Mad never used it in front of her brothers, though. They would've teased him mercilessly and he'd never be rid of it.

"PMS?" Jake asked, snagging a piece of bacon.

Mad inclined her head and Claire whooped,

hugging her. Heat crept up her neck. "All right, calm down."

Jake shook his head. "I've never seen women so cheerful about PMS."

Claire giggled and turned to Mad, a question in her eyes *could she tell Jake?*

Mad shook her head. *Not yet.*

Claire smiled, understanding in her eyes. "I'm so happy for you!"

They piled their plates with food and headed back to the great room to eat in front of the fire. A few minutes later, Park, Ty, and Alex came in. Mad waited for the recognition she craved. Even just a glimmer in his eye would satisfy her. No matter how much she wished she could be casual about hooking up with Park, she just couldn't. Her world had spun on its axis, landing in a precariously balanced place. Finally sleeping with Park meant something to her. And she hoped to him. You didn't just pretend like that never happened. Not that she expected a public declaration of love, but she expected something. A little tenderness, maybe? A hot look across the room? She didn't care that she'd said it was a onetime thing. She wanted more. And if the rough way he'd handled her in the shower was any indication—fierce and wild and hot—then he wasn't done with her either.

A niggling of doubt nagged at her. Okay, she'd

been aggressive with him in the shower, wanting him not to hold back with her. And she'd finally pushed hard enough that he pushed back, more than meeting her halfway. Once that kind of passion was turned on, it couldn't just be turned off. Right? She was pretty sure. Her stomach did a slow churn.

"Merry Christmas," Ty boomed, heading over to hug each of them in his exuberant pound-on-the-back way.

Park echoed the sentiment with a smile, but without the hugs. He carried a black garbage bag, probably full of Viv's presents. His gaze didn't meet hers.

Alex greeted them, giving her and her friends a kiss on the cheek before looking around. "Viv back yet?"

"Not yet," Mad told him.

She went to Park's side, where he now stood in front of the sparkling Christmas tree. She went up on tiptoe and kissed his clean-shaven cheek. An innocent gesture, though one she'd never had the nerve to do before. "Merry Christmas. 'Bout damn time I got to celebrate with you again."

"Good to be home," Park muttered, still not meeting her eyes. He took out the first gift and set it under the tree.

She reached for the bag. "I'll help."

He shifted away. "I got it. Go ahead and finish

your breakfast."

Stung, she returned to her friends, not bothering to mention she'd already finished eating. Clearly he didn't want her hanging around. *Chill.* She reminded herself this was brand new for him. Her feelings for him spanned years. She couldn't expect him to meet her where she was at.

Just then the rest of her friends arrived, rushing in from the cold in one happy bunch. As if they hadn't just seen each other last night, they bowled her over with exuberant hugs and happy chatter. That was how tight the Happy Endings Book Club had become. So much more than just a book club now.

They admired each other's holiday outfits, most of her friends wore red, either a dress or a sweater. Mad wore her skinny jeans, black boots, and a red long-sleeved shirt that read *I was naughty and it was worth it.* This year it was true more than most. She slid a glance over to Park, who squatted down in front of the tree, arranging the gifts for Viv. Her heart squeezed at the sight. For a guy with such crappy parents, he had a way of looking out for younger kids. Like her and now Viv. She knew without a doubt he'd be a fantastic dad. Shit.

She was jumping way ahead of herself. She tore her gaze from Park and forced herself to focus on her friends again.

"I can't wait to see who my Secret Santa is," Charlotte was saying.

"Yeah, about that," Mad started.

"Ah-ah," Claire said, cutting her off. Because Claire had insisted on being Secret Santa to all of the Happy Endings Book Club members when she'd heard about the family tradition.

Mad grinned. "It'll be awesome."

Everyone got their fill of brunch and scattered throughout the great room and the living room nearby to eat. Mad watched Park from across the great room. He was hanging with Ty as usual, acting like everything was normal. If he didn't step up soon, she knew her frustration level would rise to the point that she'd do something about it. Probably something reckless and regrettable. That was kinda her signature move. She stifled a sigh.

Her dad arrived with Claire's parents and Viv. Her dad helped Viv off with her coat and boots. Her niece yanked off her red hat with a pompom and tossed it before running to the Christmas tree. Her dark brown hair was in pigtails, messy from the hat, and she still wore her red fleece pajamas with snowflakes. "Santa!" she exclaimed.

Alex scooped her up. "That's right, pumpkin. Wait for the family. Not all of these gifts are for you."

Viv struggled mightily to get down. Alex lifted her

and blew a raspberry on her belly, making her giggle and distracting her. "Let's get you breakfast, then presents." She popped a thumb in her mouth, and he carried her into the dining room.

They returned only five minutes later, Alex trailing after Viv with a piece of toast, urging her to finish.

Everyone watched as Viv jumped up and down in front of the tree, bursting with excitement and doing a very good job of not grabbing any presents. She looked to Alex for direction and when he didn't move quickly enough, she screamed, "Daddy!"

Mad's dad appeared at her side and put an arm around her. "Reminds me of you."

"Charming and adorable?" Mad asked.

"Sure, let's go with that," her dad said. She knew she'd been hell on wheels. And so was Viv.

Alex held up a large box and read the tag. "It's for you." He set it in front of Viv, who dove right in, ripping the paper off gleefully with both hands.

"Ooh!" she exclaimed. It was a Fisher-Price airplane.

Park approached and knelt next to Viv. "You want me to set it up for you?" It must've been from Park, who'd always loved planes.

Mad blinked back the hot sting of tears, ridiculously emotional. *Pull it together.*

Viv nodded and watched as Park opened the box

and took everything out of the packaging for her. Viv immediately grabbed the girl figure and put her in the pilot seat, even though there was a boy pilot figure.

"That's my girl," Mad said, coming over to give her niece a high five, who high-fived her back, unaware she'd naturally chosen girl power.

Park glanced at Mad and quickly turned back to Viv. "It needs batteries. I'll see if I can rustle some up." He left the room.

Mad stepped away, feeling conspicuous. Alex handed Viv another present, picked up another one, and handed it to Josh. "From your Secret Santa."

"Oh yeah?" Josh took the present, shaking it and putting his ear up to it.

"You're going to break it!" Mad exclaimed.

"She gives herself away every time," Ty barked. Her brothers laughed. They always knew who she was Secret Santa for. Each of them had a way of provoking her into revealing herself. Idiots.

Josh grinned at her and opened it. "Cool. Thanks, Mad. This'll come in handy."

"That's a really nice one," Hailey put in. "We use it at cooking class sometimes." Hailey helped local chef Shane O'Hare run holiday cooking classes at Ludbury House, where she worked as a wedding planner.

"I got it on a Black Friday sale," Mad blurted. "It was just a teensy bit over the twenty-buck limit with tax. Besides, I owe Josh for all he's done for me."

Hailey looked to Josh and then to Mad curiously. "What did he do?"

"Put up with her smart mouth for years," Josh quipped. He shot Mad a look that said *drop it*.

Everyone was looking at her curiously. Mad opened her mouth to explain just a little without giving away too much, knowing Josh didn't want his twin to step in with the money and especially didn't want their dad to feel bad that he didn't have the funds. But before she could get out a single peep, Josh wrapped her in a bear hug that smushed her face into his chest and ruffled her hair. "Thanks."

Claire clapped. "Time for my gifts!" She went to the back of the tree and came up with a stack of wrapped gifts, each one in the exact shape of a book. Jake carried a large gift bag too.

"Hmm," Mad said, smoothing her hair back in place, "I can't imagine what it is."

"Just you wait," Claire said, sounding giddy. She handed a gift to each of the book club members. "Open them at the same time!"

They all opened their books. *The Princess Bride* by William Goldman.

Claire beamed. "Next October when I come back to Connecticut to film the last part of the Fierce trilogy, we'll watch the movie version together."

"Ooh, I've seen this one!" Hailey exclaimed. She had an encyclopedic knowledge of romantic movies that dated all the way back to early black-and-white screwball romantic comedies. Maybe that was where she got her old-fashioned insults for Josh.

"But we need to read the book first," Claire said. "Compare and contrast like we did with *Gone with the Wind*." The women sighed over that gloriously romantic book. Mad had been way into the dark and broody Rhett Butler, who didn't give a damn.

Claire pointed a finger at each of them. "And no cheating watching the movie without me."

They all shook their heads solemnly. It was kinda sad they could only see Claire when her shooting schedule allowed it.

"And…" Claire said dramatically, gesturing for the gift bag. Jake opened it and she handed out black T-shirts with a skull and crossbones that read I am the real Dread Pirate Roberts.

Hailey laughed. "Awesome."

"I don't get it," Mad said.

"You have to read the book," Claire said. "We'll wear it on our movie night. Or before if you're into it."

"This is all so wonderful," Hailey said. "I feel bad you got all of us a gift but we didn't get you anything. I thought I was only supposed to get one gift for my

Secret Santa."

The women had to agree.

"Awww!" Claire exclaimed. "You being here for my wedding and spending Christmas with me is the best gift in the world." She gestured to all of them, waving them close. "Group hug."

They all huddled around her and did a big squeezy hug. Mad didn't even mind that Ally squished her ribs in her enthusiasm.

"Looks like a football huddle," Jake said. "Who's calling the plays?"

"Who do you think?" Josh asked drily.

Hailey bolted upright to glare at Josh. They broke apart, the women tucking their gifts in a safe place away from the Viv tornado, who was still tearing through gifts that Alex handed her, exclaiming with glee over each one and then reaching for the next one.

Park returned with batteries and set up the plane before handing it over to Viv. It made cute noises and played a cheerful song. Viv smacked the plane once and went back to opening her presents. Park left it there and headed over to Ty.

Mad quickly joined them, anxious to see Park again mostly because it was killing her that he showed no sign of their shared night (and morning) and that was all she could think about. "I would've loved a plane like that when I was her age. Instead I got a football." She remembered the picture of her at two years old, just a little older than Viv, in an oversized football helmet, holding the ball on Christmas morning.

"No, Jake got a football and you stole it," Ty said. "You got a baby doll that you threw in the garbage."

Park laughed. "That sounds like you."

Mad jolted, a little surprised she'd gotten something that girly. She didn't remember having any dolls. Maybe because she threw them all in the garbage? "I didn't know that. Geez. Was Dad mad I threw away my gift?"

Ty shrugged. "I don't know. I just remember I thought it was hilarious. Course, I was seven. Every dumbass thing was hilarious back then."

Mad turned to Park, trying to see a glimmer of the heat they'd shared. He quickly looked away, cool and distant. She set her teeth, her frustration level rising fast. This distant Park was the one she remembered from his infrequent visits home from the Air Force. It sucked balls. Their intense hookup had been mere hours ago.

Everyone watched Viv as she helped Alex hand out presents. Mad worried her bottom lip, confused and unsure what to do about Park. This had to be the most awkward morning-after of her life. A warm hand squeezed her hand briefly. She turned and Park gave her a small smile before looking back to Viv.

She couldn't help the dopey smile that spread across her face. The joy bubbling up inside her made her want to throw her arms around his neck and kiss him. Then she had an idea.

She subtly shifted closer to Park. "I've got another present in the living room. Help me carry it?"

"Sure," Park said and followed her like a clueless stud. Not that she planned to breed with him. Not yet anyway.

She waited until she got all the way to the archway connecting the dining room to the living room, where a sprig of mistletoe hung. "Here it is."

"Where?"

She pointed up.

He looked and then his gaze locked on hers for a brief tension-filled moment. She licked her lips. His gaze dropped to her mouth.

Her pulse thrummed through her.

He looked over his shoulder in case anyone was watching. They weren't. When he turned back, she threw her arms around his neck and kissed him as she'd longed to do from the moment he'd walked in. His fingers speared through her hair, his mouth rough on hers. The heat was back and she gloried in it.

"Park?" a masculine voice called.

Park jerked away and turned, tucking Mad behind

him. She peeked around him. It was Ty coming right for them. She swallowed. Ty had a quick temper and was fiercely protective of her. Park was his best friend.

"Mad?" Ty asked, closing the distance between them.

She stepped out from behind Park. "Hey, what's up?"

Ty turned to Park. "What the hell are you doing to my sister?"

Park put his hands up. "Nothing."

"We're together," Mad said.

"We—" Park started before Ty grabbed him by the collar and hauled him up close.

"You don't mess around with Mad," Ty growled.

"Ty, let him go," Mad said. "I want to mess around with him."

Ty let go and shoved Park back. "You know the deal."

"What deal?" Mad asked, looking between the two men.

Park straightened his shirt, his jaw clenched tight.

"Not her," Ty said.

Park's lips formed a flat line. She waited for him to tell Ty to fuck off or put his arm around her or something, but he did none of that. Instead he nodded once. "I know." He left, his stride stiff, back to the cheerful festivities of their family.

Ty turned to follow him when Mad smacked his shoulder. "What the hell, Ty! This doesn't concern you."

"Park understands," Ty said and left.

She wanted to kick both men. Smash their heads together. But they were gone, having come to some kind of understanding that affected her yet shutting her out.

She ripped the mistletoe off the ceiling and threw it.

CHAPTER TWELVE

Mad drove back to Clover Park with Hailey, Charlotte, and Lauren the day after Christmas. Hailey was at the wheel of her orange Mini Cooper convertible, Mad in the passenger seat, and Charlotte and Lauren in the backseat. The car reeked of peppermint because all of them were sucking on candy canes. They'd taken Hailey's car because it was the newest and, therefore, the least likely to break down on the long drive to Maine and back. Carrie and Ally were sharing a ride in Carrie's old Toyota, named Ollie, which Carrie had an unnatural faith in. The car was at least ten years old.

"So now that we're away from the guys, spill," Charlotte said over the sound of Hailey's Harry Connick Jr. Christmas playlist.

Hailey immediately turned down the volume. The car was heavy with quiet expectation. Girl-talk time. Everyone in the car knew they meant Mad. She was the only one who'd had an agenda going into this wedding.

"Not much to tell," Mad said, which earned her a poke in the shoulder. She turned to see Lauren grinning at her, teeth tinged with pink from the candy cane.

"Your pants are on fire," Lauren said, sounding every bit the second-grade teacher she was. "I saw you two slow dancing. You could practically see the steam!"

"And I saw you looking after Viv instead of enjoying a good party," Mad returned.

"She's a sweetheart," Lauren said with a smile. "I love kids. That's why I became a teacher."

"She's not sweet," Mad said. "I love her, but she's not sweet."

"All toddlers are sweet," Lauren insisted. "With their chubby little cheeks and their little diaper waddle. And those curls!"

"You only watched her nap," Mad said. "She wasn't at full power yet."

Lauren waved that away. "I think she's great. When she woke up, she patted my cheek and called me thoo-per. I think she meant super."

"Or stupid," Mad said. "Sorry. Just putting that out there."

Charlotte pulled the candy cane out of her mouth.

"Stop trying to change the subject, Mad. What's up with the love of your life?"

Mad got serious. "I don't know. It seemed like it was going well. We hooked up, it was awesome, but one word from Ty and Park completely backed the hell off."

Charlotte's brown eyes flashed. "You tell Ty to butt out." She scowled. "That one thinks he's God's gift to women." She sucked her candy cane ferociously.

Mad faced front, feeling a little queasy and not sure if it was motion sickness or thinking about the way Park backed off.

"Ooh, Char," Hailey chortled, wagging a finger in the air. "So much fire between you two!"

"Don't even think about it," Charlotte snapped, cutting off Hailey's matchmaking tendencies. "Do you know what Ty did at the wedding reception?"

"What'd he do?" Hailey asked eagerly, peeking in the rearview mirror at Charlotte.

"Asked every single woman there to dance except me," Charlotte announced. "Even Mad."

"It's true," Mad said. "I told him to get lost. But, of course, in a more colorful way."

"Of course," Hailey said dryly.

"Do you really think he did it on purpose?" Lauren asked. "Maybe it was a coincidence. Maybe he just ran out of songs to dance to. There were a lot of us women there."

Mad turned back to shoot Lauren an exasperated look. The woman always saw the good in people and Ty had totally played Charlotte. But she didn't need to say a word.

Charlotte did a classic head swivel and turned to Lauren. "Uh-uh. This was one big dis. He knew exactly what he was doing."

"But why would he do that?" Lauren asked. "You're the best dancer of all of us."

"He's playing a game," Charlotte explained patiently. "Trying to get me to go to him."

"She's right," Mad put in. "It was his hard-to-get ploy. My brothers are idiots."

"Not all of them," Lauren put in softly. "I wouldn't have minded having a big brother to look after me. I just had my little sister. I was more like a mom to her than a sister because we're ten years apart."

"It's great until they piss you off," Mad said. "Then you just want to punch 'em."

"Oh, I could never do that," Lauren said earnestly. "Anyway, Josh and Jake are sweethearts."

Hailey snorted. "Maybe Jake."

"And Alex and Logan seemed nice," Lauren added before popping the candy cane back in her mouth. She moved so quickly her long light brown hair got caught on the sticky candy. She carefully extricated her hair.

"They have their moments," Mad conceded, turning back in her seat and sighing.

"Okay, back to Mad," Hailey said. "I think her makeover was a hit. She got his attention, drew him in, and danced."

"Don't forget hooked up," Charlotte said. She gave Mad's shoulder a shake. "Go, girl."

"Yeah," Mad muttered. "Hard to forget."

"But now we have to think about next steps," Hailey said. "We have to call off Ty, who's probably just doing his big-brother duty, and then look at how to go from hookup to an actual relationship. You could invite him to the New Year's Eve party at Garner's."

"Sure, or I could just invite him to my bed," Mad said. "We're living together until he finds a job."

"I didn't know you were living together!" Hailey exclaimed. "I thought he was just there for the weekend. He's not moving in with one of your brothers?"

"Ty lives in California, normally," Mad said. "Right now he's at a hotel in the city. Josh has a one-bedroom apartment, Alex has Viv, and Logan and Ethan share a place. Marcus is in the city. Park hates the city. Anyway, I think he wants to spend time with my dad. They're close."

"You can't expect her to make a move with her dad around," Charlotte put in.

"That could be extremely awkward for everyone," Lauren said. "Do you have a trash bag in here? I can't get my hair off my candy cane."

"No, sorry," Hailey said.

"I got it," Mad said, grabbing some napkins from her messenger bag. She reached back and snagged the candy cane, stuffing it into the side pocket of her car door.

"Hey!" Hailey protested.

"I can work around my dad," Mad said. "He works night shift and sleeps days. He's the least of the problem. Park's just so distant."

"He'll come around," Hailey said confidently, still eyeing the sticky mess in the passenger door. Her zeal for matchmaking, however, could not be denied. "This is brand-new territory for Park. He's still getting used to the fact that you're an amazing, beautiful, smart, full-grown woman."

Mad blinked rapidly. Hailey had a way of suddenly jabbing straight to the heart. "You too," Mad mumbled. "Don't worry. I'll get rid of the candy cane mess when we get home."

"Thanks!" Hailey said brightly. "But we don't want Park to keep hooking up with you because it's convenient and never branching into more intimate territory."

"We were plenty intimate," Mad quipped halfheartedly, but she knew Hailey was right. She wanted more with Park. No one had ever measured up. Truth was, she loved him. Always had. Always would. She'd never attempted a relationship with anyone else. Only Park would do.

"Now don't take this the wrong way," Charlotte started.

Mad groaned. "No good ever follows that sentence."

But then Charlotte surprised her when she directed her comment to Hailey. "How do you know so much about relationships, Hailey? Tell us about yours."

"I know a lot from my experience working closely with engaged couples," Hailey asserted.

"So you never had a relationship?" Charlotte pressed.

"I'm still very young," Hailey said.

"You think twenty-six is very young?" Charlotte asked in a tone that said *reality check*.

Hailey smiled tightly. "I need to establish my business first, create the foundation for a secure future. Believe me, when the time is right, I will search in earnest for Mr. Right."

The women fell silent.

"That's troubling," Mad finally said. "How can I

listen to your relationship advice when you've never had a relationship?"

Hailey huffed. "I told you—"

"I'm the opposite," Charlotte said with the voice of hard experience. "I've had a series of awful relationships. I finally called it quits on men three years ago."

"Do *not* tell me you haven't been with a man in three years!" Mad exclaimed.

"I've been with men on my terms," Charlotte said.

"Oh, that's what I do," Mad said.

"I used to eat my way through heartache," Charlotte said. "And then I finally said fuck it, what am I doing one hundred pounds overweight over some jerk. I got a personal trainer, changed my eating habits, and got so into it I became a personal trainer myself."

"Wow, that's so cool," Mad said, reaching back for a fist bump. Charlotte bumped her. "I never woulda guessed it. You're so trim and strong."

"Damn right," Charlotte said.

"See, isn't this great girl-bonding time?" Hailey said. "Nobody minds the tiny car, right?"

"Next we'll be braiding each other's hair," Lauren put in.

They all laughed.

"All I can say is don't make it easy on Park," Charlotte said. "In fact, make yourself scarce at home so when you do show up looking hawt as hell, he'll sit up and take notice."

"She's good," Hailey said. "But remember you want to keep wearing pretty clothes and doing your hair. You don't want him to see you as the same old Mad."

"And tell Ty to fuck off," Charlotte said.

"No one tells Ty to fuck off," Mad said. "He's a black belt. Serious muscles. Have you seen the man?"

"What's he gonna do?" Charlotte asked with a snort. "Kick Park's ass?"

"I wouldn't put it past him," Mad said.

"When's he go back to California?" Charlotte asked.

Mad lifted one shoulder up and down. "I don't know. Probably after the New Year."

"Then don't worry about him," Charlotte said. "If he gives you and Park a hard time, you come to me."

At the hard tone in Charlotte's voice, Mad turned to look at her. "And what are you going to do?"

"I'm going to level the playing field," Charlotte said ominously.

Mad got a chill. That girl was seriously fierce.

The remaining hours passed quickly as they talked about the wedding and Claire and Jake's honeymoon and where they'd each like to go for a honeymoon. Just before they got to Lauren's apartment, Lauren confessed guiltily that she'd jumped ahead and finished reading *The Princess Bride*, staying up late last night to read it.

"Lauren!" Hailey exclaimed. "You know we always read chapter one together." That was a book club tradition now. Hailey liked them to experience the story as a group from the start.

"Sorry," Lauren said, not looking too sorry. "But it was so good!"

"Okay," Hailey said. "Just wait on the movie until Claire can join us."

"It'll be tough, but I'll try," Lauren said.

"Swear it," Hailey said.

"Fine," Lauren said, all cranky like. "I swear." Clearly she wanted to jump ahead, but they all knew she'd never break a promise.

After Hailey dropped off Lauren and then Charlotte at her house near the edge of Clover Park, she headed to the downtown area of Clover Park.

"Uh, you still have to drop me off," Mad said. She lived in Eastman in the opposite direction.

"Do you mind stopping by Ludbury House with me?" Hailey's hands tightened on the steering wheel, making her fingers white. "I got a call this morning that there was a break-in on Christmas. I need to look around and report on what's missing."

Mad's jaw dropped. "You're just mentioning this

now?"

Hailey loosened her hold on the wheel and sighed. "I needed not to think about it for a while. I'm terrified, actually. Clover Park has always been so safe."

"We're getting you a security system."

"Yes, of course. I never thought we needed one before. The police said the person smashed the glass on the back door and opened it that way."

Mad blew out a breath. "Okay, no problem. I'll go with you."

Hailey glanced over. "I'm scared to go back to work after the New Year. I mean, I spend a lot of time there by myself. Sure, there's occasional cooking classes, weddings, and planning appointments, but it's also my office, and in between appointments, it's just me."

"The security system will help. And I'm teaching you self-defense."

"I'm not very athletic," Hailey said in a small voice. She forced a laugh even as her hands shook on the steering wheel. "You've seen me play basketball."

It killed her to see the usually confident Hailey reduced to trembling. "You know how you're teaching me to be pretty?"

"You're already pretty. I'm just enhancing it."

"I'm going to teach you to be a badass."

Hailey straightened, eyes wide. "You really think you can?"

"Yes," Mad said firmly.

Hailey stopped at a red light on Main Street and stared at Mad, part hopeful, part uncertain.

Mad barreled on confidently. "It will go against every bit of pageant training you've ever had. There's no room for polite manners or graceful good looks when it comes to defending yourself. You've got to hit their weak spots hard. No mercy."

Hailey's hand went to her throat. "You're scaring me."

"Your eyelash curler scares me, but I still let you near my eye."

Hailey rolled her eyes. "You knocked it out of my hand."

"So let me get near you at the dojo and then you knock me away."

"At the dojo?" Hailey screeched. "I don't know how to do karate!" She faced front, saw the light was green, and hit the accelerator hard. "Oh, gosh. This all feels like too much."

"Okay, okay. We'll take it slow. How about a self-defense class with the book club? We could just do it at the high school gym with some mats. I'll teach. Keep it simple."

"Everyone?" Hailey brightened. "Like a singles

mixer? Should we invite some single guys?"

"If they'd like to kiss the floor, then yeah."

"Oh. Maybe we'll just keep it us ladies."

"I'll find one guy to dress up in pads and helmet so we can practice on him. The bigger the better. Otherwise, sure, all girls sounds good."

Hailey launched into her usual planning mode, which made Mad smile. That was more the Hailey she knew. "I'll advertise to bring in some more single women. Maybe we can transition them from the class to our book club."

"Sure."

"This could be good," Hailey said, enthusiasm gaining in her voice.

"It will be. I'll toughen you up."

Hailey nodded. "Okay. Yeah. Tough." She bit her lower lip.

A few minutes later, Hailey pulled into the parking lot behind Ludbury House and turned off the car.

"Do you want to call the police to go in with us?" Mad asked. Not that she was worried about a break-in. She'd had them all the time in her old crappy Manhattan apartment. Usually she discovered it after they left and called the cops to report it. A few times she'd walked in on some guy looking for something valuable, but she had nothing worth shit. Just a TV. She'd bailed in a quick exit. Being the daughter of a cop, she always filed a report. Never knew if there was a pattern, maybe involving more people in the neighborhood. Anyway, they never returned. They weren't there for her and she doubted this break-in on Christmas day in a completely empty mansion had been aimed at Hailey.

Hailey stared straight ahead, a death grip on the steering wheel. "No, I don't need to call the police. They already checked on it this morning for me. No one's there. I'm just, you know, spooked."

Mad peeled Hailey's hands off the steering wheel and squeezed them. "Repeat after me. Badass babe. Badass babe." Sometimes you had to reach a person where they were at. She'd never call herself a babe. She was fierce, powerful, strong, a total badass, and she'd earned it through years of martial arts training. Eventually she'd get Hailey to think of herself the same way. It was the only way to live.

Hailey laughed. "Okay, let's go."

They went to the back porch. The police had taped over the broken panel of glass on the back door to keep the cold winter air out. Hailey unlocked the door and they stepped into a large kitchen gleaming with stainless steel appliances and a stainless steel prep table.

Hailey grabbed Mad's arm. "Stay close," she whispered.

"Yup."

Hailey gulped, an audible sound.

Mad flicked on the light. They moved slowly through the first floor of the mansion from kitchen to pantry to closets. Mad turned on lights as they moved, causing Hailey to gasp and look around wildly for intruders each time. She would've laughed if she didn't know just how scared Hailey was. They moved to the front foyer and then to the parlor next to it.

Hailey stopped in front of the parlor fireplace. "The candlesticks are gone!" she exclaimed in a loud whisper. "They were silver, original to the house!" Ludbury House dated back more than a hundred years.

Mad spoke at a normal volume. "Maybe you should write this stuff down. Do you have pictures of them somewhere?"

Hailey stared at the empty spot where the candlesticks used to be for a long moment before turning back to Mad. "You know, I probably do from all the small weddings that happened in here. The larger ones go in the front foyer with the grand staircase or outside. They'd be in my office."

Hailey headed confidently out of the room, across the hardwood foyer to her office on the other side. Mad followed and Hailey scribbled a note on a legal pad.

"Your laptop's still here and the printer," Mad

said.

Hailey stopped and stared. "That's good. But wouldn't they make more money selling electronics than antiques?"

"Maybe they didn't make it to this room before they had to bail. No one ever said criminals are smart."

Hailey bit her lip, her pale blue eyes worried again.

"We need to check upstairs." When Hailey didn't move, Mad took the lead. "I'll go."

"No, wait! I'll go with you."

They went up the grand staircase to the former bedrooms now made into dressing rooms for the bridal party. A few rooms were completely empty. Nothing seemed to be missing. Mad turned off the lights again and they returned downstairs, stopping in the foyer.

Hailey's brows furrowed. "All they took was the candlesticks. I find that more troubling than if they ransacked the place." She crossed her arms and shivered. "It's strange. Isn't that strange?"

"Maybe it was a homeless person who just needed somewhere warm to crash for the night. They took the candlesticks for a little quick cash for their next meal."

"A meal," Hailey said. "That makes sense. Let's check the refrigerator."

They headed back to the kitchen. Hailey flung open the refrigerator door. Six yogurts and an assortment of condiments. Hailey just stood there and stared.

"So?" Mad prompted. "Anything missing?"

Hailey slowly shut the refrigerator door and turned. "They ate my salad and roast chicken. I was waiting to throw it out until the garbage guy returned after Christmas. I didn't want to leave it out in the garbage and have the raccoons get into it." She wrung her hands together. "Oh, this is so sad. We should help this person."

"We should report this person."

"Mad!"

"No," Mad said firmly. "You have to report them. What if he or she shows up again? What if they're mentally unstable and feel threatened by you being here? You don't know what you're dealing with. We have to report all this and make sure it doesn't happen again."

Hailey bit her lip. "I guess."

"And then we've got one week to turn you into a badass."

"One week!"

She jerked her chin. "You reopen after the New Year, right? That's one week."

"I can't possibly learn self-defense that quickly."

Mad ran her fingers through her hair and shook her head for the confidently tousled look. "I learned to be beautiful in a week, right?"

Hailey looked extremely doubtful. Mad narrowed

her eyes and Hailey rushed to agree. "Absolutely!" she exclaimed, though not very convincingly.

Mad put her hands on her hips, glad they'd settled things here. "All right, then. You get the word out to book club and anyone else you think might be interested in self-defense, and I'll reserve some gym time. I'm thinking Thursday afternoon since most of us have off this week. Maybe Saturday morning too. Sunday we party for New Year's Eve. Sound good?"

Hailey traced the tile of the kitchen floor with the toe of one velvet boot. "You really think you can get gym time that quick?"

"I have connections. We'll ask Chief O'Hare when you make your report. He has the keys to the high school. Maybe he'll even want to help teach."

Hailey chewed on her fingernail. This was disturbing because Mad knew Hailey never liked to ruin her nail polish.

"Babe power!" Mad said, holding up a fist for a fist bump.

Hailey reluctantly released her fingernail. "Babe power," she said a lot less enthusiastically. Her return fist bump was more like a soft nudge.

Mad made Hailey's fist connect a little more forcefully.

"Ow," Hailey complained.

Mad sighed. "We'll work on it."

CHAPTER THIRTEEN

Park drove back from Maine with Ty on Friday after spending a few extra days hanging out at Claire's cabin, hoping the distance from Mad would help him cool off. He wished he'd had time to buy a car stateside because driving with Ty was irritating as all hell. It took a lot to get Park angry and Ty had just about got him there.

"All I'm saying is, you don't mess around with Mad," Ty said for the fifth time since they'd left Maine. Park was counting.

"Nobody messes with Mad," Park said tightly. "She can take care of herself."

"If our friendship…" Ty paused, "if our family means anything to you—"

"It means everything!" Park slapped a hand on the dashboard of the rented sedan. "Why do I still have to prove I'm worthy? Like any minute you guys are going to change your mind about me and give me the boot."

Ty ignored that. "I know you've always had a soft spot for her and that's why, back then and now, I told you she was off-limits." The very first time Mad had caught Park's attention at the town pool as a teen in a swimsuit, Ty had issued a very believable threat of bodily harm that put a quick end to Park's quiet admiration. Then Ty had followed up his threat with a deal Park believed he had no choice but to accept.

"Not her," Ty had said. "She's not someone you mess around with and then dump. You want to keep your place with our family, then you treat her like family *and that's it*. Deal?"

The Campbells meant too much to Park to ever risk losing his place with them. "Deal," he said, earning a quick bro handshake. An overwhelming relief ran through him that his continued place in the Campbell family was no longer on shaky ground.

Now Ty was back on the same track, reminding him why Mad was off-limits. "She's not some girl you hook up with and dump."

"What if I don't dump her?" Park asked. He felt accused and tried before he'd even had a chance. He knew he came from a crappy situation—his mom a junkie, his dad an alcoholic, his baby sister dead—but he'd grown up. His sister's death had been called "crib death," though he suspected it was neglect. So, yeah, he'd been pissed off as a kid and used his fists for a long time, but he'd worked hard to be better than that. He'd have a good job soon. Was he really that awful? Too low to be with the adored Campbell little sister?

"You gonna marry her?" Ty asked.

He pressed his lips together. He knew he wasn't marriage material.

"Didn't think so," Ty said like he was onto Park's nefarious intentions. Never mind that Mad had seduced him. Park wouldn't have gone there otherwise, no matter how tempted he was. Mad deserved better than him, he'd always known it, and Ty knew it too.

Ty just wouldn't let it go. "If you're not gonna marry her, if it's not serious, then hands off. I won't stand by and watch you bail and break her heart again."

Park startled. "What? What do you mean again?"

"She was devastated when you left for the Air Force."

That hit him like a slap. "I know you said it was tough on her, but everyone was leaving. She was the youngest; it was inevitable."

"No, it was different with you. It took her years…God, she'd kill me for saying this. Forget I said that. Marry her or cut her loose. It's that simple."

"You know I'm not cut out to be a family man."

"That's what she deserves and, if you care about

her at all, move on. There's plenty of women out there you can hook up with."

Park glared out the front window, pissed off yet knowing Ty was right. He wasn't serious about her. Wasn't serious about anyone. He didn't think he ever could be. He told himself it was for the better. He'd find a new place to crash as soon as possible so he wouldn't be tempted living in the same house with her.

Ty socked his arm. "Glad we understand each other."

Park said nothing.

"You know I'm going easy on you, right? I really wanted to kick your ass when—"

"Got it," he said through his teeth, annoyed that Ty kept harping on the same point. "You're the big brother." And she was a grown woman who knew what she wanted. He'd never forget she wanted him to be her first. It meant a lot to him, even if he wasn't, just knowing she'd chosen him.

"You used to look out for her too." Ty scrubbed a hand over his face. "Ah, hell, I don't want to think about it. Moving on. Why don't you meet up with me in California after the New Year? I'll introduce you around. I'm sure we could get you some work."

"I'll let you know," Park said, accepting the peace offering. "I'm applying a bunch of places. I'd like to work on planes if I can. Use what I know."

"If you wanted to work on planes, then why'd you leave the Air Force?"

He'd been tired of being shipped off to the desert, tired of being in war zones, missing home. Especially since Mad's texts and emails had been less and less the last couple of years. He understood, she was juggling working and going to school, but he hadn't realized how much that tie to home had sustained him until it was gone.

"Guess I was just ready for a change," Park said. "Ready to come home."

"Was it tough over there? I don't even know some of the places you've been."

Park filled him in on what he could, the early mornings, the late nights, all the volunteer 365-day deployments he'd signed up for in classified locations for the extra hazard pay. It wasn't just enemy fire they had to worry about, either; friendly fire from young recruits blowing off steam while they waited to be called to duty was also a danger. He was proud of his part in serving his country. His main goal, always, was to strive to be the man Joe Campbell raised him to be. A lofty goal, one he feared he could never quite reach with all his damage.

Ty told him all about the stunt work he did out in LA and sometimes in New York City or Vancouver.

Exciting stuff, but Park found his mind wandering as thoughts of Mad and their night together flashed through his mind. That tattoo. He still couldn't believe she'd matched him, right over her heart. Like she wanted to be reminded of him forever. Didn't she know he was a bad bet?

By the time they arrived back home in Eastman, Park had convinced himself he was not the man for Mad. He'd explain it to her and hopefully she would understand. She might get pissy, but she'd cool off eventually. Then they'd go back to being friends.

Ty dropped him off with one last warning. "Don't forget what I said."

He bit back the snarky remark he wanted to say, *how could I when you won't shut up about it?* He gave a curt nod, exited the car, and let himself in the house. At least Ty was staying in a hotel in the city and wouldn't be in his face about Mad all the time.

She appeared at the top of the stairs and flashed a wide smile. His heart beat loud in his ears, the message harsh and insistent, *danger, danger, danger.*

"You're back," she said, heading down the stairs toward him.

He stayed frozen in place, hands at his sides. Her clothes were baggy—T-shirt with cargo shorts—and should not be tempting in the least, but his body was on high alert because he knew in exquisite detail the perfection underneath.

"Hey, little bit," he said to remind himself as much as her what she'd always been to him. His pip-squeak to look out for.

"Hey, big guy," she said in a voice dripping with innuendo as she sauntered over to him, making a big show at looking at his cock. She *had* noticed he was hung earlier. His cock rose in appreciation of the compliment.

No, wait. He wasn't supposed to like that. He took off his leather jacket and casually held it in front of him.

She smirked. Yeah, she noticed. "Have a good time with the guys?" Her black T-shirt read Try Me and it was damn hard not to take that as an invitation.

"It was all right."

She stopped directly in front of him. Up close she was all glossy and shiny. Her hair was in soft waves, she wore makeup that made her doe-brown eyes look wider, her cheeks and lips were rosy like she'd just had an orgasm. He clamped down on that thought and looked upstairs, away from her.

"Your dad home?" he asked. It was seven o'clock. He wasn't sure if he was working over Christmas break.

"Left for work an hour ago," she said, taking his jacket and tossing it on the sofa. She turned back, getting close enough for him to feel the heat of her sexy little body. Her T-shirt had a small V where she'd ripped the collar, revealing part of the tattoo that might as well have been his name. His fingers tingled, aching to trace the hawk over her heart. He pulled his gaze from it with great effort, sliding to her collarbone, up her slender throat, to her pointy chin.

"We gonna talk about this or just go for it?" she asked.

His gaze snapped to hers. "I don't know what you mean."

She wrapped her arms around his neck and pressed her petite frame against him, all curves and strength. "We slept together."

He peeled her off him with a groan. Leave it to Mad to boldly announce it. "That can't happen again."

Her eyes flashed. "Why not? We're two consenting adults and we have the house to ourselves."

"Ty—"

"Fuck Ty." She lifted her chin, all belligerence, her legs shoulder-width apart in battle mode. This was a battle he couldn't win. Either way, sleep with her or deny her, he'd screw things up for himself with the Campbell family.

He took a deep breath. "Okay, *I* don't want to mess things up. I'm not...I don't do relationships.

Mad, you know…" His voice choked, his throat tight.

"Know what?" she snapped.

He cleared his throat. "You've always been special to me."

She softened and took a step closer. He backed up a step.

"That's a start," she said.

"I don't want to hurt you."

"You won't. I won't let you."

He glanced toward the door. "Look, I'll get a hotel or something."

She blew out a breath. "It's a three-bedroom house. There's plenty of room for both of us. It's not like I can't control myself." She met his eyes and frowned.

He so wanted to fix this. He didn't want to fight or piss her off. He wanted to spend time with her again. Like they used to. He'd missed her so much for far too long.

"Can we go back to what we had before?" he asked. "Pretend it never happened."

She stared at him like he was nuts. "Seriously?"

He pulled her in for a hug. "Sorry, that was a stupid thing to say. I'm just trying to make it easier."

Her arms wrapped around his waist and she rested her head on his chest.

The least he could do was comfort her. He stroked her soft hair, glad she wasn't too mad. Hopefully things would go back to normal soon.

Finally she lifted her head, and his heart lurched at the pain he saw in her eyes. She went up on tiptoe, her face tilted up at him. He froze. Her lips brushed across his, the soft touch luring him in. Still he hesitated. His body said go; his brain said stop.

She did it again, grazing his lips with another soft, teasing touch.

"Mad." He had nothing more. Just Mad. His brain was shutting down.

Their eyes met for a long sizzling moment.

"Park," she whispered.

He crushed her to him, deepening the kiss, the attraction too strong to deny. His mind clouded; there was nothing but her soft mouth, the heat, the undeniable pull to bring her closer. He lost himself in the kiss, his hands stealing under the back of her shirt, needing to feel skin. But it wasn't enough. He backed her up against the wall, pressing his body fully against hers, his mouth claiming hers. Her hands were all over him. Red haze of lust. Intense. Overwhelming. Then she was unbuttoning his jeans. Oh God. He lasted ten minutes resisting her. What was he doing?

He grabbed her wrist, stilling her hand. She broke

the kiss, twisted out of his grip, and met his eyes, breathing hard. They both were. Fuck. Maybe he should get a hotel.

He held up a hand. "I think—"

"Don't think."

He shoved a hand in his hair. "I'm going to go up. Got some things to do." Like take care of this boner.

"Fine by me," she said in a surprisingly agreeable tone.

He started toward the stairs and she kept up with him. He stopped. "Just me," he ordered. "Mad, please."

"I made a lot of effort to look nice for you tonight," she said through her teeth. "I let Hailey do my hair."

"You look nice," he said, a little surprised she was fussing over her hair. That wasn't like her. "Your hair is nice." He found himself smiling because it was also kinda nice that she'd made an effort for him. Even if it wasn't something he could follow up on.

She put her hands on her hips, always a sign she was pissed. "And Charlotte did my makeup, but that's not good enough for you. I'll never be one of those petite girly girls you like. You can just say it. I'm not your type."

He regarded her for one solemn moment, saw the easiest way to shut this overwhelming thing between them down, and took it. "You're right. You're not my type."

She sucked in air and staggered back.

He immediately stepped forward, reaching for her, but she jerked away. He wanted to take it back, wanted to spare her tender feelings. "Mad, time out, wait—"

"Screw you, Parker Shaw." Her voice was quiet and deadly calm, which somehow made it worse. "You don't deserve me."

He pressed his lips together, unable to deny it. "You're right."

She turned and crossed to the front door, opening it to the frigid cold of a December night.

He couldn't help himself. "Take a coat; it's cold."

Her shoulders moved up and down like she took a deep breath and then she left.

He scrubbed a hand over his face. It was for the best, he told himself. He'd done the right thing. Except everything about this felt wrong. He couldn't relax and found himself sitting on the sofa in front of the TV for hours, listening for her return. Finally, near midnight the door opened again. At the sight of her, whole and healthy, he finally relaxed. He knew it didn't make sense. She'd been on her own for years, far away from him, but now that he was home, he felt tied to her again and needed to know she was okay.

He stood and crossed to her, wanting to make amends. He hadn't meant she wasn't his type. Far from it. "About before, you know…well, I hope you know…" He trailed off at the death glare she aimed at him.

"Glad you're home," he said to her retreating back as she headed upstairs.

He hated that he'd hurt her.

"Mad!" he called. "I didn't mean…" He stood there for a moment and was about to follow her upstairs, but then he heard the shower running. Visions of a naked Mad in the shower flashed through his brain. That last time in Maine when he'd joined her in the shower. She'd been aggressive, pushing and pushing him until he couldn't hold back his natural aggression anymore. He'd taken her too roughly, focused only on the dark urgings of his own body, only dimly aware of the noises she made. He didn't even know if she was okay until he'd finished and her hoarse voice finally penetrated the lusty haze of his brain.

He flopped back on the sofa and turned up the volume on the TV, trying to drown out the sound of the shower. It was his own damn fault. He never should've caved to baser instinct. He had to think first, then take action.

Yes, that was the problem. He hadn't stopped to think it through. He wouldn't make that mistake again.

CHAPTER FOURTEEN

Park sat in the kitchen with a cup of coffee early the next morning. His dad came in a few minutes later, off work from his night shift as a security guard.

"Morning," his dad said, grabbing an apple from the fruit bowl.

"Morning."

"How you adjusting to civilian life?"

"It's a little weird not to have a schedule, but…" He trailed off as Mad walked in, looking all pissy. Her eye makeup was gone, her red hair rumpled and sticking up. She wore a V-neck undershirt that was too big for her and baggy sweats. He tried not to think too hard on why that was appealing. It was probably the wing of the hawk tattoo peeking out of the shirt that had his undivided attention.

"Hi," she said, getting herself some coffee.

"Morning, sunshine," her dad said. "Who pissed you off?"

She dropped a piece of bread in the toaster and pressed the toaster lever down. "I'm fine."

Park quickly looked away.

His dad joined him at the table, rubbed the apple on the front of his shirt, and took a bite. A few minutes later, Mad joined them, chomping her toast. She met his eyes across the table and glared. He shifted his gaze to his coffee.

"There a problem I should know about?" his dad asked, looking at Mad and then Park.

"I don't have a problem," Mad said, looking right at Park.

"No problem here," Park said, looking only at his dad.

His dad looked back and forth between them for a moment. "Yeah, okay."

An awkward silence fell.

After he finished his apple, his dad stood. "Welp, I know this might be hard to believe, but I have a date for New Year's."

"Who?" Mad asked. "Where did you meet her?" Park wondered the same thing. His dad hadn't been on a date in years.

"Let me just see how it goes," his dad said. "I'll be heading out tonight for Boston and I'll be back on the second. Don't burn the house down while I'm gone."

Park studied him, thinking it extremely odd that

his dad had a date at all, let alone a long-weekend kind of date. Did he suspect Park and Mad had hooked up? Was this his way of giving them a chance to be alone?

His dad smiled, his expression giving nothing away. "I'm going to shower and head to bed."

Park waited until he left before turning his gaze back to Mad.

She smiled, one of her scary smiles that communicated dangerous intent. "Could you go to my women's self-defense class in an hour?"

"So you can whale on me? No, thanks."

"So the other women can practice on you. We need someone big."

He leaned back in his seat. "Go find another big guy."

"But you're the perfect guy for the job."

No comment. He knew she was pissed and would like nothing better than to have an excuse to let that out.

"Fine, stay here, then," she said. "I'll just tell the women you were too scared."

"Yup."

She frowned, probably because she didn't get a rise out of him, and headed upstairs. He stayed downstairs and got on his dad's laptop to work on his résumé and comb job sites for something that would fit. At some point he heard the front door open and close without a word of goodbye. She'd get over it. They'd go back to normal soon.

Mad stayed away all day. Soon it was night and his dad left to visit his friend in Boston for the long weekend. Park hadn't been able to get any details out of him either. Very odd.

He didn't know where Mad went or who she was with and didn't relax until she finally returned home late that night. She glared at him where he sat on the living room sofa and went upstairs. He hadn't been waiting up for her. He really couldn't help it if the only TV in the house was near the front door.

The next day, New Year's Eve, dragged. Mad went out with her friends right after breakfast. He finished his résumé, emailed it to Josh, who had a good eye for detail, and then sent it out to a bunch of places.

Time dragged by.

And by.

Were the clocks broken? It seemed like it should've been later than it was. He did a quick check around the house, but they seemed to be all synchronized to the same time.

Just him and the TV for company. He tried not to jump at every little noise that might be the front door. He was only watching TV on the living room sofa because it was comfortable. He wasn't waiting for her to come home.

Finally she returned, all soft looking again. Her hair softly waved, her makeup like she'd just orgasmed—stop it! Her clothes tight, her tattoo peeking out of a fuzzy blue V-neck sweater. He was beginning to suspect she was purposely showing off her tattoo, knowing how much it got to him.

He turned down the volume on the TV and worked out a compliment that would still keep her in the friends box. "You look nice, mini."

She lifted her chin. "It's not for you, if that's what you're thinking. I'm going to a New Year's Eve party at Garner's tonight."

"Oh." He'd been kinda hoping they'd have New Year's Eve together at home. Josh was working the party at Garner's. His other brothers had plans, some of them working, some of them out of town visiting friends. He should've made plans too. What was he waiting around here for? He supposed he could see what Ty was up to in the city tonight.

She stood in front of the TV, where he couldn't help but get a good view of the hawk wing, the clingy sweater, the tight jeans, and badass boots. "You can come if you want," she said, and then blew out a big gust of air like she was doing him a *huge* favor. "I guess," she added.

He slouched further into the sofa. "Gee, what an invitation. Can't wait."

She narrowed her eyes. "You hit on any of my friends and you're dead."

"Duly noted. Okay to hang with Josh?"

"He's going to be busy. He's not just the bartender, you know. He's manager now."

"So I guess I'll hang with you if that's okay."

She lifted a shoulder. "Whatever. Just don't give me a hard time about my drinking or my behavior or whatever."

He straightened. "No comment on whatever." He stared at her mouth, that full lower lip tempting him again with its softness. He met her eyes, his voice gruff. "I'll go easy on you tonight."

Their gazes locked in a tense standoff. He didn't realize he was holding his breath until she finally spoke.

"We leave at seven," she said tersely.

He leaned forward. "Are you ever going to stop being mad at me?"

Her mouth worked, like she was sucking a lemon, before she said, "Don't be late."

~ ~ ~

"Mad!" Hailey hollered and rushed over for a big hug the moment Mad arrived at Garner's. Mad blew long Hailey hair out of her mouth. She was still getting used to all of Hailey's warm hugs.

"And Park!" Hailey said, giving him a quick hug. "Happy New Year! C'mon, grab a drink!" Hailey danced her way over to the dark cherrywood bar.

Mad followed. "You hit the bar already?"

"I did! Josh here finally had all the ingredients for my fave." She leaned across the bartop and smiled goofily at Josh. "Right, Josh? The delivery finally got straightened out."

Josh bit back a grin, his brown eyes full of good humor. "Right, princess." He slid a mojito with a mint leaf sticking out of it in front of Hailey.

She beamed at him. "Thank you," she said with a surprising amount of warmth. She took a big slurping sip. "Ooh!" She put a hand on her head. "I got tiaras. Tonight I really will be a princess. We all will." Hailey grabbed Mad's arm and squeezed. "Wait here."

She strode off unsteadily to a corner of the restaurant where she must've stashed them.

Park leaned against the bar, his eyes half-hooded. "You really gonna wear a tiara?"

She bristled. "Why not? I'm not girly enough to be a princess?"

Park lifted one shoulder and turned to Josh. "Can I get a Corona?"

"I'll have scotch," Mad said. "The good stuff."

"You got it," Josh said, fetching the beer.

"You drink scotch?" Park asked.

Mad set her teeth, tired of the way the men in her life judged her every move. "Watch me."

Park straightened to his full height and glowered down at her. "Isn't it a little early to start with the hard stuff?"

She gave him a long, obvious once-over. "I like hard stuff."

Josh choked on a laugh before serving up the beer with a slice of lime. "Better watch yourself, Park."

"What's that supposed to mean?" Mad asked.

Josh went to get her scotch. He returned and poured a small amount in a tumbler. "Ty told me to keep an eye on him." He jerked his chin at Park. "But I'm thinking maybe I need to keep an eye on you." He set the scotch in front of her.

Mad sipped her drink rather than snap at Josh. He'd done too much for her to tell him to fuck off, even if she wanted to.

Josh pointed to his own eyes with two fingers and back to her.

Whatever. He had his eye on her. So did all of her big overprotective brothers. Even now she could feel Park's eyes on her, probably all set to take the next drink out of her hands because he'd deemed she'd had enough. She shook out her shoulders. Fuck 'em. Tonight was for fun.

"Mad, over here!" Hailey said, waving wildly.

Park gave Mad a small salute. "Time for your tiara."

She sensed sarcasm and ignored it, joining her friends where they were gathered around Hailey, who held a large shopping bag. "For you, princess Charlotte," Hailey said, presenting a plastic silver tiara to Charlotte.

Charlotte put it on. "Now where to find a prince?"

The women laughed.

Hailey distributed them to the others. Her friends looked super cute—Lauren, Carrie, Ally, and newcomers Missy, Sabrina, and Lexi too. Hailey had an impressive way of making friends. They'd just met Missy, Sabrina, and Lexi last Thursday for the first time at self-defense class. They'd returned to the Saturday self-defense class, where everyone was considerably more amped up, and now here they were celebrating New Year's Eve together. She had to think it was more than Hailey just wanting to find new clients for her wedding planning business. More than being an overly romantic matchmaker. She just loved people and loved connecting the people she met to each other.

"Quite a group you got here," Mad told Hailey. "Here." She handed the tiara back. She knew she could never pull off the princess look.

"Oh, you," Hailey said, settling the tiara on Mad's

head for her. "We're Happy Endings Book Club sisters in solidarity."

Mad got a lump in her throat. How many times had she wished for a sister? Now she had the book club and, legally by marriage, Claire too. "Does it look weird on me?"

"Just a minute," Hailey said, adjusting the tiara and fussing with Mad's hair. "There."

"You look cute!" Lauren said. She pulled out her cell, took a picture, and showed Mad. Huh. She didn't look as weird as she'd thought. In fact, she kinda blended with the other women. She never thought she could fit in so easily. Why did she always feel so different? It was like her awkward teen years when she'd tried and failed to be one of the girls was constantly biting her in the ass.

"Let's mingle!" Hailey said, linking her arm with Mad's and pulling her along.

Hailey was a natural at working a room. She brought Mad and the whole group along with her, introducing them to people they didn't know. She seemed to know everyone in Clover Park. Well, she had grown up there. Mad listened as Hailey told everyone about the Happy Endings Book Club and all the great books they'd read there as well as her work as a wedding planner. The word of mouth for Hailey's business, based on her motormouth, must be amazing, but Mad started thinking of what else Hailey could do to expand. Some of her new marketing knowledge filtered through her head, coming up with new ways to get the word out. She'd mention it once Hailey was sober again. The woman was exuberantly happy-tipsy right now.

Mad felt someone staring and looked over to see Park leaning against the bar, watching her. He jerked his chin at her in acknowledgment. She returned the gesture.

"Girl, he's been staring at you all night," Charlotte said, fanning herself.

"No, he hasn't." Mad felt her cheeks heat. "He said I'm not his type."

"What?" Hailey exclaimed.

"Shh," Mad said.

"That is ridiculous!" Hailey practically shouted. "You're everybody's type!"

"Geez, keep your voice down," Mad said.

Hailey went on as if she hadn't heard her. "A smart, confident, educated woman. If he doesn't see that—"

"Yeah, I think he's a liar," Ally put in. She cupped a hand near her mouth and said in a stage whisper, "He's checking out your ass right now."

Mad stiffened. For real? She peeked over her shoulder at Park, who turned to say something to Josh.

"You guys," Mad said, completely exasperated, "I know you're just trying to make me feel better. He likes petite girly girls. That's not me."

"You look petite to me," Lauren said. She was kinda tall, at least four inches taller than Mad.

"To me too," Charlotte said, who was nearly as tall as Lauren.

Ally grinned. "I'm petite and you're my size."

Hailey threw an arm around Mad's shoulders. "And you're definitely pretty when you're not scowling."

Mad scowled.

"Turn that frown upside down," Carrie, a sweet nurse with glasses, quipped, doing a big exaggerated frown-to-smile gesture that nearly made her tip her white wine.

Missy Higgins, a brunette in her twenties and a new member of the group, put a hand on her hip. "I don't get why women have to be smiling all the time. Maybe I don't feel like smiling. Does that make me a bitch?"

"No," the women chorused.

"I have a scary resting bitch face," Charlotte said, giving them a dead-eye stare. "I like it that way."

Missy gave her a fist bump.

"But you look cute when you smile," Hailey said to Missy, completely missing the point. Hard to fight years of pageant training. "How do you like Clover Park?" Missy was new to town and the sister-in-law of a former book club member.

"I like it," Missy said. "I got a good start with the Marino family sort of taking me in. I go to all the Sunday family dinners with Nico and Lily." That was Missy's sister. "Plus I met these two at the apartment complex." She turned to smile at Sabrina and Lexi.

"And we're awesome," Sabrina said, lifting one hand in the air.

"True dat," Lexi agreed. They toasted each other, clinking their plastic glasses of champagne.

"You should definitely flirt with Park," Charlotte said. "He's into you for sure. See where things go."

"I don't know how to flirt," Mad muttered.

"Ah," Hailey said, "my specialty. It's a dance. You lean in, pull back, give him a chance to lean toward you. Yes?"

Mad stared at her blankly. "I have no idea what you mean and I'm a terrible dancer."

"I'll show you." Hailey smiled sweetly and leaned close to Mad. "Hi. Great party."

Mad backed off. "Don't flirt with me. Show me with a guy."

Hailey flicked her hair over one shoulder. "Okay. Pick one."

Mad looked around. Most of the men seemed to

be with someone. Of course, there was Josh, but that wasn't really a fair example. He liked to mess with Hailey too much to go along with it. Then she zeroed in on a guy in his thirties, dark hair parted to the side, and a wide grin.

She pointed. "That guy."

Hailey looked over. "Ooh, he's the mailman. Terrible choice. He asks out everyone." She looked around. "You see? This is why I need to import single men to Clover Park. Everyone here is married except us."

Mad pulled out her cell. "Let me see if I can rustle up some guys. She texted all of her brothers, even Alex, though she figured he was probably home with his young daughter. Ten minutes later, she hooked one. "Ethan just got off his shift. He'll be here soon. He's a cop in Eastman."

"You mean the one with—" Hailey gestured to her stomach in a rippling move "—the twelve-pack abs?"

Mad laughed. "I guess. Is there such a thing as a twelve-pack?"

Hailey nodded. "Oh yeah. I remember from the basketball game." Hailey had joined the guys in one of their Saturday basketball games. They'd played shirts versus skins and Hailey had been mesmerized by a couple of the shirtless guys.

"That was more than a year ago," Mad said with a

laugh.

"Burned in my brain!" Hailey exclaimed, eyes wide.

Everyone laughed. They chatted for a while, making multiple toasts to each other, the new year, being a badass, and the Happy Endings Book Club. She caught Park staring at her. He gestured to her tiara and gave her a thumbs-up. She quickly took it off, suspecting he was making fun of her.

A moment later Park appeared at her side. "What're you doing taking it off? You looked very sparkly in it." He grinned.

She scowled. "Shut up."

Park turned to Hailey. "She's mad at me."

Mad squirmed.

"And why is she mad at you?" Hailey caroled with a gleeful smile plastered on her face.

Park raised a brow at Mad. Like she was really going to tell everyone that he refused to sleep with her again. It sucked to be friend-zoned and she wanted out of that zone as soon as possible.

"I'm not mad at him." *I'm hurt, stung…yeah, I'm pissed.* He said she wasn't his type and that really stuck in her craw because she'd always secretly feared she could never match what he wanted.

Park gave her a disbelieving look.

Her friends sort of wandered away. Park studied

her.

"What?" she practically snarled.

He pushed a lock of hair behind her ear. "Truce, okay?" Before she could get out another lie about being just fine, he leaned down to her ear, the stubble of his cheek brushing against her. "I take it back. I only said you weren't my type because I needed us to go back to being friends."

"Really?" she asked, floored.

He kept talking, the words hot against her skin. "I miss you around the house, miss you in my life. Spend time with me again."

He straightened, seeming to be waiting for her to say something.

"I will. I—" she swallowed over the lump in her throat "—miss you too. But why..." She trailed off as a large hand landed on her head and mussed her hair like it was sucking on her head. Ethan Case.

He moved to her side. Everything about him was sharp—dirty blond hair with spikes in front, hard blue eyes, chiseled cheekbones—softened by his full lips that occasionally cracked a smile. Like now. "Brain sucker and it's starving."

"Ha-ha," she said, shoving his hand off her head.

Ethan pulled her head close and kissed the top of it. "Happy New Year, shortstack."

Her friends gathered in close again, eager to flirt

with Ethan.

Park snatched the tiara from her hand and settled it back on her head. "Royalty suits you."

She stared at him, speechless.

"And we're her royal friends," Hailey chirped.

Ethan laughed. "Nice to see you all again." He scanned the group. "Some of you are new to me." He went over and introduced himself to the new women. Then he took them all in, a small smirk on his face. Some women found that smirk sexy. Mad had no idea why. "I remember most of you from the wedding. Especially you, Charlotte." He bumped Charlotte with his hip. "You got the moves on the dance floor."

Hailey laughed. "I wish I had a chance to dance with you too."

Ethan turned, a smile slowly spreading across his face. "Oh yeah?"

Hailey hid a smile by sipping her mojito, her eyes lighting up. "Yup."

Ethan crossed to Hailey, getting close enough to whisper in her ear.

"Maybe later," Hailey said.

Ethan held out a hand. "Or maybe right now."

Hailey looked to Mad and raised her brows in a gesture of *and that is how you do it.*

Hailey took Ethan's hand and he turned her in a slow twirl and brought her close, his arm wrapped around her waist. He leaned down and smiled at her.

"Yo, Eth!" Josh called from behind the bar. "Want a beer?"

Ethan looked over at him. "You paying?" He grinned down at Hailey, who beamed back as he twirled her back around.

"Yeah," Josh called.

"Come take my place," Ethan said to Josh. "I can't leave the woman hanging mid-dance."

Mad choked on a laugh. Ethan was onto Josh and calling him on it.

Josh raised his palms. "Can't leave my post."

Hailey put her hand on Ethan's arm. "Another time. Thanks."

Ethan took them all in. "Ladies, excuse me, I could use a beer. Long day with a bunch of nuts. Thankfully I didn't get the late shift. That's when the real crazies come out."

"Like us," Mad said.

Ethan laughed. He snagged Park, one hand on the back of his neck, and brought him along to the bar.

Hailey finished her mojito with a big *aah*. "And that, my dear Madison, is how flirting is done." She did a big twirling flourish with her hand. "Your turn."

"So let me get this straight, I'm just supposed to go over there, mimic your performance, and wait for your critique?"

Hailey beamed. "Exactly."

"At least she's honest," Charlotte put in.

Mad squared her shoulders and marched over to the bar, her tiara firmly in place. "Can I get another scotch?"

"Yup," Josh said, serving it up.

Ethan and Park were talking to each other a short distance away, paying her no mind.

She reached for the glass, but Josh held it. She met his eyes. "What?"

"Sip it. You've still got two hours until midnight."

"I binged on fried chicken earlier. It's absorbing all the alcohol."

"Over at Jimmy's?"

"Yeah."

"I told you that stuff is crap." Josh was a foodie and disapproved of fast food. Sometimes comfort food hit the spot, though. She'd gone by herself, quietly enjoying the decadent meal of fried chicken, French fries, fried corn bread, and coleslaw. The past couple of days had been rough for her, trying to come to terms with the fact that she wasn't Park's type. Why did he say that if it wasn't true? He was usually so careful of her feelings.

She looked over to where Park and Ethan stood and back to Josh, who still held her drink hostage. "Can I please have my drink?"

He let go. "Fine. Start your New Year with a hangover."

She saw the caring in his deep brown eyes and caved. "Okay, I'll sip," she said on a sigh. She had to pick her battles with her overprotective brothers.

He dipped his head and went to help another customer.

She shifted over to Park and Ethan. "Charlotte wants a turn dancing with you, Eth."

Ethan raised a brow. "Never keep a lady waiting." He strolled over and took Charlotte's hand, who looked surprised for a moment but then quickly went with it.

Mad set her scotch on the bar and turned to Park. "Why did you say I wasn't your type?"

He leaned close, keeping his voice low. "I told you already. I need us to be just friends. Sorry I hurt your feelings."

She relaxed a little, feeling more like the Park she knew had returned. He was one of the few men who ever noticed when her feelings were hurt. "So why do we have to be just friends?" She needed a real answer. One that made sense to her. Otherwise they were wasting time when they could be together.

He stared straight ahead, his jaw tight. "We've always been friends."

"And then we weren't," she said evenly.

He turned back to her. "And now we are again."

She took a deep breath and caught Hailey smiling encouragingly at her. She turned back to Park, who gave her an *isn't it great to be friends again* smile. She silently seethed, her temper pushing her to one of her signature reckless and regrettable moves.

"And that's all we're going to be?" she asked.

"What do you think of the Patriots' chances of going to the Super Bowl?" he countered.

It was a question she found hard to resist. They'd always been hardcore football fans at her house. They launched into a long discussion of football that had Park downright animated. She enjoyed herself despite the fact they weren't exactly moving things to where she'd hoped.

Finally the topic wore itself out. Ethan returned and Park asked him about his latest arrests.

Mad let out a long breath, worn out from the roller coaster of her emotions, grabbed her barely touched scotch, and headed back to her friends. They were gathered in a group, talking and laughing. All of that stopped when she returned and they all looked at her expectantly.

"Good job!" Hailey exclaimed.

"Don't get too excited," Mad said. "He just wants to be friends."

"Friends is a great start," Lauren said. "You guys

are living together. It'll happen. Just give it time."

"Why are you always so sweet?" Mad asked. "Nothing ever bothers you."

Lauren's green eyes widened. "I was just trying to help."

"Sorry," Mad said. "I'm just not good at being patient and taking things slow."

"Look at it this way," Ally put in, "if your goal is to marry him, you'll have your whole life together."

Says the woman who ran away at the altar. None of her friends had any good relationship experience that would help her.

"I didn't say I wanted to marry him," Mad said in a fierce whisper. "Why does everyone assume women want to get married?"

"You don't?" Hailey asked.

Mad looked over at Park, the only man she'd ever loved, and lied through her teeth. "I don't." It hurt too much to wish for things that would never happen. All that hurt quickly turned to anger. She tried to push it down, tried to enjoy hanging with her friends, but every time she looked at Park yukking it up with Josh and Ethan, completely content to treat her like one of the guys, *a pal,* denying everything they'd shared that meant so much to her, she teetered closer to the edge of control.

By midnight, she was dancing on a table, her

friends cheering her on, Josh yelling at her to get down, and Ethan smirking. She raised her arms over her head, which made her sweater lift, showing off her nice innie belly button, and added some hip action for a super-sexy dance. She flashed a grin when Park's gaze finally connected with hers, which quickly died when he strode straight for her, his expression fierce and determined.

Next thing she knew Park was carrying her out the front door, her body flung over his shoulder. She would've cheered if she didn't feel so dizzy.

Happy New Year to me.

CHAPTER FIFTEEN

Park put a steadying arm around Mad as he guided her upstairs to her room. She was drunk and went from quiet in the car to all soft and sweet the moment they entered the house. He wasn't one of those guys who found drunkenness all that appealing. His home life pre-Campbell drove that home. And while he appreciated her sexy dance, he didn't appreciate everyone else getting an eyeful of her.

"Happy New Year to me," she sang.

"Happy New Year to you," he replied, guiding her down the hallway.

"To us," she said with a goofy smile.

He moved her along quickly, practically carrying her, and pushed her into bed. It was a queen-size bed, the bunk beds that used to be there long gone. She lay flat on her back, unmoving. He undid the ties on her boots, pulled them off, and set them on the floor.

He gazed at her for a moment, a small smile on her

face, her entire body relaxed. "Sleep this off and I'll see you next year."

"Ha!" she said. "See you next year. Ah, bed."

He pulled the covers over her and she pushed them off.

"My jeans are too tight," she informed him. Before he could stop her, she was peeling them off. He quickly looked away and turned to go.

"Help!"

He stifled a groan, turned, and looked. She was kicking and struggling with the jeans caught around her ankles. She wore purple boy shorts panties. So perfectly Mad.

He grabbed the jeans, trying not to touch the bare skin of her legs, and quickly slid them off. She stretched out those toned sexy legs and wiggled her feet.

"You hate my panties, don't you?" she asked. "But they're so comfortable."

"Night, little bit."

"I'll take them off." She grabbed the sides of the panties and he put his hands over hers to stop her.

"They're awesome. Keep 'em on."

She placed his hands flat against her hips. "Feel how soft they are."

He dutifully stroked the fabric over her hip, a safe zone of sorts. "Yup."

She sighed and pulled the cover over herself, curled on her side, and slept.

He made a quick exit, turning off the light. He stood in the hallway for a moment and blew out a breath. He knew he'd dodged a bullet. She'd been all over him tonight, talking to him about all his favorite stuff in a way that few women could, her sexy little body leaning close, her fresh citrusy scent washing over him. He trudged across the hall to his room.

The next morning he woke to the unmistakable sound of retching. He went into the hallway to make sure she'd made it to the bathroom. She had. Maybe now she'd learn her lesson about drinking too much.

He went downstairs to start the coffee, made some toast, and waited. An hour passed and no sign of Mad. Finally she appeared, freshly showered. She drank some coffee, declined food, and returned to bed.

He kinda missed her company, but he figured she needed to sleep. The house was so quiet. Her dad wasn't due home until tomorrow. He decided to visit Ty, who was leaving tomorrow. He returned that night with some take-out Chinese. "Mad, you here? I got your favorite, pork lo mein."

No reply.

He went upstairs to hear her moaning in the bathroom. The door was closed. "Mad, you okay?"

She retched. He winced. That sounded really bad.

"Go away. I'm sick," she said in a weak voice.

He stood there for a minute, unsure how to help her. "You still hungover?"

"It's much worse than that. I think I have food poisoning. Please go away."

"Okay, call me if you need anything."

He went downstairs and put the TV on while he ate at the coffee table, half of him still listening for signs of life upstairs. He checked on her a few times. Still in the bathroom. By the time it was late enough for bed, he was alarmed to find she hadn't left the bathroom. "Mad?"

She moaned.

"Do you need a doctor?"

"No."

"Have you had anything to eat or drink today?"

"I can't."

He leaned against the door, speaking through it. "You want some help getting to bed?"

"I'm never leaving this toilet."

"I'll get you some Gatorade or soda or something. You must be dehydrated by now."

No reply.

He bolted downstairs, grabbed her car keys, and drove to the store. He made it back twenty minutes later, poured her a glass of ginger ale and a glass of Gatorade and put them both on her nightstand.

He returned to the bathroom door. "Let me help you to bed. You need to at least sip a drink. You've been in there all day."

The door sprang open suddenly. Her hair was a tangled mess in a lopsided messy bun. Her eyes had smeared mascara under them. She was pale and shaky, wearing only a T-shirt and her purple boy shorts panties. She was basically a mess. Every part of his being reached out to her in that moment, wanting to take care of her.

He reached for her, guided her back to her room, and it hit him that maybe his desire to take care of her meant that he could be a family man. Maybe he wasn't damaged beyond hope. Wasn't that what her dad did? Took care of all of them?

"Don't look at me," she said. "I'm hideous."

"You're just sick," he countered.

She continued in silence and collapsed on the bed. He knew she must be in really bad shape if she didn't even have a snarky comeback.

He tucked the pillow under her head better. "I'm going to get you another pillow so you can sit up and drink." He headed to the door.

"Get a trash can too," she called. "Oh God." She raced past him and back to the bathroom.

It was a long night. Her petite body racked with the food poisoning. She moaned and retched and raced to the bathroom for hours.

By dawn, she had nothing left in her. Just dry heaves. He sat in a chair next to her bed, keeping vigil, putting a cool washcloth to her forehead, helping her sip flat soda.

She finally fell into an exhausted sleep. He slept in the chair by her side, one hand covering hers.

~ ~ ~

Mad woke the next morning feeling drained but relieved not to be nauseous anymore. It had to be the fried chicken dinner she'd snarfed before the party. Maybe the coleslaw; it had tasted sort of sour. She hadn't had anything but tortilla chips at Garner's. Josh was right. That junk-food stuff was poison. Her stomach muscles hurt, her throat burned, and her tongue felt fuzzy. So gross.

She slowly turned her head to see Park asleep in a chair next to her bed. He'd seen everything. Seen her at her worst. After all the effort she'd made to look sexy for him. Now he'd never see her as anything but that disgusting barfing girl.

She slowly sat up and swung her legs over the side of the bed, accidentally bumping one of his long legs.

He jolted. "Hey, you're awake. How're you feeling?"

"Shitty."

"You need help getting to the bathroom?"

Tears stung her eyes. The room smelled like barf. "I didn't want you to see me like this."

"It was pretty bad, but you pulled through."

Her frustration and weakened state crumbled her control and she found herself crying. She crossed her arms, hugging her middle, which still hurt like hell.

"Hey, hey." Park shifted to sit next to her and put an arm around her heaving shoulders. "It's okay. Take a shower, brush your teeth, and you'll start feeling human again."

She was beyond embarrassed. She was mortified.

"How can you stand to be near me?" she asked.

He brushed her tangled hair back. "You needed me."

She wiped her eyes. "Thank you. I'm going to try to clean up."

"I'll air out your room for you."

She bit her wobbly lower lip and moved on unsteady legs to the door. A strong arm wrapped around her, helping her there. She managed, slowly and with frequent breaks, to brush her teeth and take a shower. When she returned to her bedroom, clean sheets and a new comforter were on the bed. It smelled fresh too like cold winter air.

She couldn't even…there were no words for her level of gratitude. She would not cry again. He had dark circles under his eyes from staying up all night with her.

He met her halfway and helped her back to bed, tucking the covers around her, brushing her hair back from her face and kissing her forehead. She suddenly felt like the little twerp he *had* to take care of.

"You always going to see me as a twerp?" she asked.

"No."

"Park—"

"Get some sleep."

"I just want to say thank you. You went above and beyond the call of duty here."

His brows drew together, his expression uncertain. "Did I do a good job taking care of you?"

She couldn't believe he even asked that question. "Yes. You did a great job."

He put a hand on her shoulder and squeezed. "That means a lot to me. Rest up."

She was extraordinarily tired. She curled on her side, felt his hand on her head for a long moment like a blessing, and drifted to sleep.

Two days later, Thursday, Mad felt better, enough to eat and drink normally. Park had been sort of fussing over her. It was sweet, but she still felt mortified. After he'd seen her in such a hideous state, she went back to her normal clothes, no hair styling, no makeup. There was just no way to come back from barfing girl. He'd never be able to get those images of her in the throes of food poisoning out of his mind. Nothing sexy about her, as was evidenced by the fact that he never touched her, never flirted, despite the fact they spent plenty of time together alone at home. Her dad was home now but back to working the night shift.

She and Park were sitting on the sofa, binge-watching *Supernatural* since he'd missed a lot of TV when he was overseas. Her cell rang. Hailey. Park paused the show for her.

Hailey's voice was high and fast. "There was another break-in at Ludbury House."

"Oh shit. What'd they take this time?"

"I don't know. I'm afraid to go look. The police gave me the all clear, but…" Her voice faded out.

"Are you in the car?" Mad asked.

Hailey's voice came back loud and clear. "Yes. The security system is supposed to be installed next week. Mad, I don't want to go to work tomorrow."

"Do you have to?"

"I have three appointments, but I can't! It's like the place is haunted or something. I feel all jumpy like someone is just waiting around the corner or hiding in a closet."

"Remember you're strong, you're fierce—"

"I'm not you."

"You did great in self-defense class."

"We've only had two classes. I'd hardly call myself qualified to face off with an intruder."

"I'll go with you tomorrow. You'll be fine, I promise."

"Thanks, Mad."

She hung up to find Park staring at her. "What?"

"What're you doing for Hailey?"

"Just checking out Hailey's work with her after someone stole something. The police already gave the all clear."

His hazel eyes narrowed. "Wherever you're going, I'm going with you."

She rolled her eyes. "I'm a black belt."

"Don't care."

"I've fended off men twice my size at the bar I used to work at in the city."

Park blanched. "Geez, Mad, what happened to you? When I left you were an honor student. Then no college—"

"I went back."

"Why were you working some crap bar where you had to defend yourself?"

She tried to grab the remote, but he held it out of reach. "Answer the question," he ordered.

"Because of you, okay?"

His head reared back. "Me? But I told you to study hard and stay in school."

Her throat got tight. Fine. She'd put it all out there. She had absolutely nothing left to lose at this point. "Because I was devastated when you left," she said quietly. "I couldn't eat, couldn't sleep." She met his eyes. "You broke my heart."

His brows scrunched together. "You were fifteen."

"My heart didn't care," she choked out. She dashed at her eyes with a fist. Dammit. She'd told herself she wouldn't cry over Park anymore.

His arms wrapped around her, his hand cupping her head against his chest. His voice came out low and soothing. "I wish I could redo all that for you. It was like we weren't ready for each other then. I needed to make a man of myself, to prove I could. You weren't even technically an adult."

"And now?"

His hand dropped from her head and he gazed down at her. He cupped her cheek and her breath caught. Was it possible that he could want her after all that he'd seen? That he could look past all that and see her on the inside?

There was a knock at the door. Mad heaved a sigh. "To be continued."

She crossed to the door and peeked through the glass on the side. Hailey. She flung open the door.

"Your timing sucks."

"I'm sorry," Hailey said, dashing inside. "I know you didn't invite me, but I feel so creeped out. I just didn't want to be alone tonight." She glanced over to the sofa. "Hi, Park."

"Hi. You want me to go check things out?"

Hailey wrung her hands together. "Would you?"

He stood.

"No," Mad said. "You and I will go tomorrow when you need to get to work. You'll be fine. You said the cops gave you the all clear."

Hailey gestured to Park. "But he's so nice and big."

"I don't mind," Park said.

"She's fine," Mad said.

Hailey pulled a DVD of *The Princess Bride* from her purse. "I brought a movie."

"Isn't it cheating to watch the movie before the book?" Mad asked.

"I already read the book."

"Hailey! I'm surprised at you. Weren't you the one who gave Lauren a hard time for skipping ahead? We're supposed to read chapter one together." Hailey was very insistent on the group experiencing the start of a book together. She'd even postponed the book club meeting until next Thursday since Mad had been so sick. She probably could've gone, but she hadn't been sure before today.

Hailey bit her lip. "I need to watch something happy."

"Oh, fine. Just don't tell the others."

"Like I would." She handed the DVD to Mad, who set it up.

"You want to watch?" Hailey asked Park.

"Sure."

Mad thought that was awfully sweet of him considering they were right in the middle of *Supernatural* season two.

The three of them sat on the sofa, watching the movie. Mad sat between Park and Hailey. It was actually a great movie. They all laughed a lot. By the time the credits rolled, it was late.

"Can I stay a little longer?" Hailey asked.

"You can have the couch if you want," Mad offered.

"Great!" Hailey said brightly. "I'll just get my overnight bag from the car."

She rushed out the door to get it.

Park raised a brow at Mad, and she couldn't help but laugh.

~ ~ ~

The next morning Mad agreed to drive with Hailey to make sure everything was okay at her work. It was early. They'd go in, do the all clear, and Hailey would drive her home. Her friend didn't want to be alone for one moment, even in the car. She was that freaked out.

Mad ordered Park to stay behind when he tried to follow. "You need to get used to the fact that I'll still be alive without your help," Mad told him. "Seriously. This is an important milestone in our relationship."

"You guys have a relationship now?" Hailey asked.

"Sort of," Mad said. "He's still afraid to touch me."

Park hauled her up against his side. "Who's afraid?" he asked, giving her a kiss on the cheek. Lame. But she didn't push him away.

"You guys are so cute!" Hailey exclaimed.

"Yeah. Cute." She eyed Park, who stared back at her, a gleam in his eye. "See ya, Park."

Once in the car, Hailey yammered on a mile a minute the way she did when she was nervous. Mad wasn't nervous at all. First of all, the robber would have to be an idiot to make an appearance in broad daylight. Second, he or she probably just needed someplace warm to spend the night.

Hailey parked in back, still babbling on about who knew what. Mad tuned her out as all of her stilled, focused on the task at hand.

Mad made a shushing gesture. "Be cool," she told Hailey.

"Should we sneak in the back or go through the front door?" Hailey whispered.

"Good idea. Let's sneak in the back. That way if someone's there, we can surprise them. Get out your cell phone to take a picture."

Hailey's hand went to her throat. "You really think the robber is in there?"

"No, but I hope so. I want to catch him or her in the act."

"Wait. First let's check the perimeter."

Mad rolled her eyes but followed Hailey around the entire mansion. Everything seemed to be locked up tight. Hailey always made sure of it.

They got to the side of the house and stopped dead in their tracks where a curtain blew gently through an open window.

Chapter Sixteen

"Maybe we should call the police," Hailey whispered.

Mad shook her head. She went up on tiptoe, lifted the curtain, and peeked inside. It was the dining room off the kitchen with only a table and chairs in the center of the room. She turned to Hailey. "I think they just left in a hurry last night and forgot to shut it."

"Wouldn't the police shut it?"

"Maybe it wasn't obvious. I mean, it was dark."

Hailey shivered. "I'm getting a bad feeling."

"You want to go back to your car and call the police?"

Hailey nodded.

"Go ahead. I'm going in." She put her hand out. "Give me the key."

"Mad, I can't leave you alone in there!"

"Then come with me."

They snuck around to the back door. Hailey unlocked it and they slowly stepped inside. Hailey reached for the light switch, but Mad stopped her. If there was someone there, she wanted the element of surprise. They tiptoed over to the dark dining room with the open window.

Empty.

Mad went over to shut the window and locked it. She pulled out her cell, set the flashlight app, and peered around the dim space. Nothing.

"We'll go room to room and see what's missing," Mad said, flicking on the overhead light.

They did a tour of the downstairs—nothing was out of place—and finished in Hailey's office.

"My laptop's missing," Hailey fretted.

Mad relaxed. "That's actually more normal than stealing candlesticks. You have a backup of all your important work stuff?"

"Of course. I print everything important and leave the duplicates at my place. Never screw up a bride's special day. My calendar synchs to my phone."

"Okay, we'll report that to the police and the insurance should cover it. Let's check upstairs."

They toured the mostly empty rooms, opening closets at Hailey's insistence, finding everything untouched.

"See?" Mad said. "Completely normal. Now you can report the missing laptop and go back to being your happy wedding planner self."

Hailey gave her a small sheepish smile. "I guess my imagination got the better of me. Thanks for putting up with me last night and today."

"No problem."

Hailey went downstairs to her office, where she called to report the missing laptop. Mad wandered back to the kitchen, curious if the fridge was emptied. She opened the refrigerator door and a large hand covered her mouth from behind. She immediately bit that hand, elbowed backward, and twisted out of the hold.

It was a man with long stringy brown hair and a trench coat.

"We already called the cops," Mad said.

He grabbed a blender off the counter and threw it at her, hurrying toward the back door. She kicked his feet out from under him, and he hit the floor, immediately twisting to grab her ankle.

She went down, hitting her head on the side of the stainless steel prep table. She saw stars for a moment. Her vision cleared. The man held a pocketknife, not huge, maybe a three-inch blade, but the crazy gleam in his eyes had her scrambling to her feet.

"Back off!" she hollered at the top of her lungs so Hailey would hear.

He lunged forward and she sidestepped him easily. She whirled, maneuvering around the prep table to the stove. She grabbed an iron skillet off the stove and felt her cargo shorts snag tight by her left knee. She glanced down to see he'd thrown the knife, which stuck out of the huge side pocket of her shorts. *Thanks for handing over your weapon.* She dropped the skillet on the stove within reach, twisted and bent to yank out the knife when the man rushed her. Off-balance from her position, her head and shoulder took the impact, slamming to the floor. Light exploded behind her eyelids and then everything went black.

~ ~ ~

Park drove to Ludbury House in Mad's car, checking up on her even though she told him not to. He didn't care that she was a black belt. She was a petite thing still recovering from a serious bout of food poisoning. Call him overprotective or paranoid, he didn't care just as long as she was safe.

He was on Main Street, about a block away, when a gut-deep sense that she was in trouble had him hitting the accelerator. Adrenaline surged through him as he got closer. By the time he pulled into the back parking lot, every part of him was on high alert. He leaped out of the car and raced to the back door. Through the glass he took in a nightmare scene— Mad's body sprawled on the floor, a gleaming knife next to her, and a large man going through her pockets. Raw anguished fury sent him bursting through the door, barreling toward the man, who looked up in surprise before he backed away. Park leaped over Mad, knocked the guy to the ground, leapt on top of him and pummeled him with his fists in a red haze of rage.

Someone was calling him, someone far away, but he couldn't stop.

"Park!" the voice rang out, reaching him clear as day. Mad. She was alive.

The haze cleared. He looked down. The guy had a bloody nose but was conscious.

The man spat in his face. "You're ugly and you'll burn in hell."

"Shut up," Park snapped, grabbing him by the hair and slamming his head into the floor. The man slumped unconscious. Park quickly got off him, kicked the knife away, and rushed to where Mad was now sitting up. He wiped his face with his sleeve. "Where are you hurt? Are you bleeding?"

She got to her feet, wincing. "I hit my head, but otherwise I'm fine."

He crushed her to him, nearly collapsing with relief. His heart thumped a glorious halleluiah. *Alive. Alive. Alive.*

A bloodcurdling scream snapped him back to reality. He whirled to face the threat, tucking Mad behind him. But it was just Hailey screaming at the top of her lungs, staring at the unconscious man on the floor.

"Call nine-one-one," he told her.

She nodded in a jerky fashion, pulled out her cell, and dialed.

"Stay here," he told Mad.

"Park—" Mad started.

"We'll talk later." He stood next to the man, wishing he had some way to restrain him until the cops arrived.

"Now what?" Hailey asked in a high-pitched voice. "What if he comes to?"

"You have any rope?" he asked.

Her brows scrunched together in concentration before she said excitedly, "I used twisty red rope to tie the greenery to the front banister!" She raced to get it.

A few minutes later, Hailey returned with several hanks of rope, all of them too short to tie the guy's wrists together. He glanced at the guy. Still out cold. "Any leftover rope longer than this?"

She smacked her forehead. "Duh. It's in the back storage closet." She headed out the other side of the kitchen and returned with it. He rolled the guy to his stomach and tied his wrists behind him.

Chief O'Hare and his deputy came, slapped some handcuffs on the man, and talked to them while the guy was still unconscious. Hailey promised to follow them to the station for a full report. They hauled him away.

Finally his worst nightmare was over. He walked Mad back to her car in silence. She thanked him, but he couldn't even speak. Now that the danger had passed and he knew she was okay, the full force of what just happened hit him in a wave of nauseating anguish. He could've lost her. Gone forever. Gone, gone, gone. Like his baby sister.

He sat in the driver's side, silent and still, staring out the front window, not really seeing anything.

She put a hand on his arm and squeezed. "You want me to drive?"

He slowly turned to her, reaching out with one shaking hand to stroke her cheek. She covered his hand and pressed it against her cheek.

"I'm okay," she said.

His voice came out hoarse. "How can you take chances like that, Mad? You're a little thing just getting over being sick. Don't you care what happens to you?"

"I thought Hailey was overreacting. How was I supposed to know? The cops gave the all clear."

He took a long shaky breath. "How do you expect us to have a future together when you take chances like this?"

Her eyes widened. "A future?"

"Yes!"

"You mean you're not just taking care of me because I'm that little twerp you always have to look out for?"

"No." He cupped her face with both hands. "Don't ever do that to me again. Not alone. I'm your backup. You got that?"

"Yes."

He gripped her shoulders, the pure anguish in his heart pouring out in a rush of words. "I can't bear it if anything happened to you."

"Park, it's okay. I'm okay."

He needed to hold her, to feel her safe and sound. He shifted the seat back and hauled her into his lap, tucking her sideways against him. She rested her head against his chest. "I know this sounds crazy, but I've always had a tight connection with you. I knew you were in trouble before I saw it. And then..." He swallowed hard. "My baby sister died and there was nothing I could do about it."

She lifted her head. "I didn't know you had a sister."

"Her name was Maya and she didn't live to see her first birthday."

"I'm so sorry."

"I guess your dad didn't want to burden you with

my fucked-up home life."

"What happened?"

He stroked her hair absently, his memories somehow more bearable with her in his arms. "They said it was crib death, but I always suspected it was neglect. You know about my parents, both of them addicts. Different poisons, same crappy results. I was in school by then, kindergarten. I guess I was lucky to have school when my parents got worse. Anyway I came home and the police were there asking questions. And she was just *gone*." His hand stilled. "I didn't even get to say goodbye. Five years later, I'm living with your dad and there's this loud sassy little girl. I put everything I had into keeping you alive, like I couldn't do for my little sister."

She stroked his cheek, looking up at him. "Is that why you always treated me so nice when all the guys told me to scram?"

He gave her a small smile. "I didn't want you to feel left out, but, yeah, part of it was I needed to keep a close eye on you to keep you alive."

"Then why'd you leave?"

"I had to."

"No, you didn't."

Knowing how painful his departure had been on her, seeing even now the pain in her eyes, he leaned down and kissed her gently. At the soft touch of her lips, desire shot through him and he deepened the kiss, reveling in her softness, her heat, her taste, reveling in the affirmation of life. He rested his forehead on hers. "I didn't know what to do with the attraction I felt for you. I couldn't chance ruining things with the family who took me in. And I knew we were both too young."

"You mean I was your type even back then?"

He kissed her. "You are the only type. Why do you think I always went out with petite girls? They reminded me of you." He smiled at the look of shock on her face. "And now I realize I've been waiting my whole life for us to be ready for each other."

She gazed into his eyes. "I love you, Park, I always have."

He brushed his thumb across her lips. "I love you too. But it changed, it's deeper now, real and raw."

"I like real and raw." A note of sexy temptress was in her voice, and as much as he wanted to go there, now was not the time.

He carefully shifted her off his lap. "Buckle up. I'm getting you checked out at the emergency room." He started the car.

"Seriously?" she asked, clicking her seatbelt. "This is nothing."

He pulled out of the lot. "Then it'll be a quick visit."

She was silent.

He glanced over to find her looking irritated. "Only because I love you so much."

"Park," she said softly, actually blushing. Mad was not a blusher.

This could be to his advantage.

~ ~ ~

By the time Mad got home, all checked out and perfectly fine, she couldn't wait to be with Park. He'd shared so much with her, stuff she'd never known, and now all his restraint where she was concerned made perfect sense. She held the knowledge close to her heart, amazed that it had always been her for him. Just like it had always been Park for her.

"Wait for me on the sofa," Park ordered before heading upstairs. She figured he was checking if her dad was home. He returned a few minutes later and joined her. "He's sleeping."

"Good."

He grabbed her suddenly, surprising her, and hauled her into his lap. He burrowed his nose in her hair and then kissed her temple.

She looked up at him. "I had no idea you were such a cuddler."

He stroked her cheek. "I'm just so glad you're alive. I love you so damn much."

"Park." She felt her cheeks heat. There was something so intensely intimate when he expressed his feelings. After not knowing for so long where she stood, well, it was almost an embarrassment of lovey-dovey mushy stuff. "I love you too."

He gazed deep into her eyes like he was looking into her soul. She felt breathless. He smiled. "I love that look in your eyes like you worship me. It's a good look for you."

"I can't believe I was your type all this time!" she blurted. "I thought I wasn't pretty enough or girly—"

"You're more than pretty." He kissed her nose. "And it's all natural, inside-out beautiful."

Her cheeks burned with all the mushy stuff coming her way. "When did you get so poetic?"

He brushed his thumb across her lower lip. "When I realized just how much I love you."

Her eyes got hot with tears. Her cheeks were still hot too.

He grinned. "You're adorable when you blush."

She nipped his neck and then kissed him roughly. "I want to make you blush now. Let's go upstairs."

He stroked her hair back. "Maybe we should wait. Your head—"

"Is fine. Let's do the shower. That was hot. I want your big thick—" She shut up when Park's mouth slammed over hers. *Yes!* The intensity ratcheted up quick, urgent need racing through her. His hand slid into her hair, his other hand under her shirt, skimming up her spine. Oh, God, she needed a lot more. Right now. She tore her mouth away. "Naked. Now. Shower."

He stilled. "I was too rough with you then. I want to make love to you."

She pulled him back for another kiss and nipped his bottom lip. "Believe me, I liked it. I told you I can handle you. I'm not going to break."

His gaze was pure heat. "You make me lose my mind. All I think about is taking, not giving."

"When you take, it's like giving. Promise." She got off his lap, stood, and tugged his hand. "Come on."

He didn't budge. "Don't you want sweet words and tenderness?"

"Yes, after you fuck me so hard I see stars."

"I want more for you," he said, stubbornly staying on the sofa. "I can control myself better in a bed."

She rolled her eyes. "And I want a strong man not afraid to take what he wants."

He shot off the sofa. "I think you just insulted my manhood."

She wiggled her fingers in a come and get me gesture. "Show me what you got."

He scooped her up in his arms and carried her upstairs. "You asked for it."

She giggled, which really wasn't like her, but she felt almost giddy. She gazed up at him, loving the intensity in his expression that she now knew meant not just lust but deep emotion.

He stopped abruptly in the hallway outside the bathroom door. "We got company." He set her down and put an arm around her waist. "Hi."

She turned, expecting to see her dad, but it wasn't just her dad. It was her dad and a beautiful petite blond-haired blue-eyed woman wearing a red silk robe. She'd never, ever seen her dad have a woman spend the night. At least her dad was dressed.

"Park?" her dad asked. "Mad? Are you two—"

"I love her, sir," Park said, his voice ringing out loud and clear, nearly making the awkward situation bearable.

Her dad cracked a smile. "Now that is good news."

Park let out an audible breath and gave her a little squeeze.

"Aren't you going to introduce us to your lady friend?" Mad asked.

Her dad got serious. "Mad, this is Tina, your mother."

CHAPTER SEVENTEEN

Mad's head reared back. "I'm sorry. What? It sounded like you just said my mother?"

The woman approached—they were the same size except the other woman had large breasts and curvy hips—and studied Mad. She turned back to Mad's dad. "She definitely took after your side."

Mad stood there, staring in shock at the woman who'd left Mad when she was only one. She'd seen pictures, but she had no memory of her in real life. "What're you doing here?" She couldn't even work up any anger. It was so surreal after the day she had to see the woman, Tina, actually standing in front of her.

"I know it's been a long time," Tina said quietly. "I was too ashamed to face you all."

"Tina reached out to me," her dad said, "and I brought her home." That was what he did, brought home people that needed his love and guidance. But that was not what Tina deserved. The woman abandoned her six children.

"Dad? Are you with her?"

He inclined his head.

"You're *with* this deadbeat?" Her voice rose in volume, but she didn't care. "She abandoned her kids and you! And you just take her back *now* when no one needs her around at all?"

"I know this must be a shock," her dad said calmly. "Let's go downstairs, have a cup of coffee, and talk."

"I won't be saying a word until she leaves," Mad said.

"It's okay, Joe," Tina said. "I'll go."

"Stay here while I talk to Mad," her dad said.

Tina retreated to the bathroom, quietly shutting the door behind her.

Park looked at her sympathetically. They headed downstairs and settled at the round oak kitchen table.

Her dad blew out a breath. "Coffee?"

"No, thanks," Mad said. Park shook his head.

Her dad folded his hands on the table. "So I guess you have a lot of questions."

"How can you bring her *here* to our house?" Mad asked.

"This was her house once," her dad said.

Mad scowled. "She has no right."

Park spoke up. "Was that why you went to Boston

for New Year's?"

"Yes."

Mad's tangled emotions and the enormity of her day turned to one fiery focus—that woman did not belong here. She had no right. She seriously wanted to kick someone's ass. Park took her hand under the table and squeezed. She took a calming breath, but it did nothing.

"So she called you after twenty-five years and suddenly wanted you back?" Mad asked.

"Her husband left her," her dad said. "She called and wondered if we could catch up."

"Catch up?" she asked, incredulous. "How about catching her up on the fact that she completely missed our childhood?"

"There's no excuse," her dad said. "She defined herself by her beauty for so long. She was Miss Connecticut, you know. But being a mom isn't glamorous. She had severe postpartum depression. And I guess she just missed her old lifestyle."

"Lifestyle!" Mad exclaimed. "Just dropped the family lifestyle, huh? Picked up a new better one."

Her dad leaned close. "My kids mean everything to me. You know that. I love you to the moon and back. She loves you too—"

"That is not love," Mad said, her voice shaking with rage.

"She was too ashamed to return," her dad said. "She doesn't think she deserves forgiveness."

Mad pounded a fist on the table. "She's right."

A moment passed in silence while she tried to pull herself together. *Deep breaths, find your calm center.*

Her dad went on. "You have a right to be angry. Absolutely. But, Mad, I never stopped loving her. And I wanted to at least try to bridge the gap between you and her and your brothers too."

How would her life have been different if her mom had taught her how to be like her? A beauty queen, like Hailey, who was so good at connecting with people. All of her insecurities came flooding back.

Mad lowered her voice, finding the words hurt too much to say at full volume. "You heard her say I took after your side like it was a bad thing."

"It's a great thing," Park put in. "You got the best genes."

But she didn't believe him.

"Just give her a chance," her dad said. "Talk to her."

Mad shook her head. "Do *not* ask me to do that. She doesn't deserve it. And you deserve better."

Her dad's gaze was direct. "I devoted my life to you kids and I don't regret that for a minute, but now I have a second chance."

She stood abruptly and headed out of the kitchen,

intent on packing up and crashing on someone's sofa because she could not stay in the same house as that woman.

"Mad," Park called.

"Let her cool off," her dad said.

She went to her room and packed a suitcase. She stopped and stared at it. What the hell was she doing? That woman should leave, not her. This was Mad's home. She dumped out the suitcase again and then threw it across the room.

"Hi," a soft feminine voice said from the doorway.

"I have nothing to say to you," Mad said.

"I'm sorry if seeing me upsets you."

She glared at the woman. Tina. She refused to think of her as her mother. "It doesn't upset me. You mean nothing to me."

"Okay, that's understandable."

"Why now?"

"Your dad was always so good to me. A gentleman."

"You'd better leave. I seriously want to throttle you."

"How did you get so abrasive? Were there no women around here at all?"

"No! It was me with older brothers and a cop dad, so sorry if I didn't turn out all girly like you."

"I didn't mean—"

"Get out of that doorway before I plow you down."

Tina backed up and Mad moved past her, hands in fists. She headed downstairs, full of so much pent-up energy she didn't know what to do with it.

"Park!"

He appeared a moment later from the kitchen.

"We're going to a hotel."

"Yup."

She hadn't thought it would be that easy. "Let's go."

"You want to pack a bag or—"

"We don't need clothes."

"Got it."

They left.

~ ~ ~

She fucked him nine ways to Sunday. All she wanted was rough wild animal sex and he gave it to her. It was the only thing that calmed her. Exactly the distraction she needed. But after an entire weekend of that— Monday morning meant back to her college classes— Park insisted on one last slow and tender lovemaking.

He leaned on his elbows and looked down at her. "No more angry sex."

She wrapped her ankles high around his waist. "I wasn't angry with you."

He brushed her hair back, kissed her eyebrows, her closed eyes, her nose, and finally her mouth. "You were getting out all that energy and now I want you to receive some of my good energy." He kissed her again, slow and deep. "My loving energy."

Park's love went straight to her heart and squeezed. The upheaval from suddenly gaining Park and then that woman showing up and ruining everything pushed Mad into a deep well of emotion.

He levered down to place a kiss on her hawk tattoo. She hoped he couldn't feel the frantic beat of her heart.

He returned to her mouth and then hovered over her, watching her as he continued a maddeningly slow screw.

"Come on," she said, bucking her hips against him. "I need more."

He spoke against her lips. "I love you."

She closed her eyes, trying to hold the tears back. "I know."

"So now I'm going to show you."

She tensed, about to break the connection and reverse their positions, when he pinned her wrists over her head.

"Let me," he said.

She could have easily broken free, but she let him, relaxing in the hold, her energy controlled.

He made love to her in a way she'd never experienced.

A union of souls.

His intense hazel eyes gazing into hers.

Sharing a breath and then another.

And then it was building inside of her, this wave of emotion and pleasure tightly tied together.

"Yes," he urged her on. "Stay with me."

She broke, an explosion of pleasure that made her let go of it all, every tight hold she had on her emotions, tears silently streaming down her face. He followed a moment after and dropped his head next to hers, breathing heavily.

Finally he lifted his head. "Mad," he said tenderly and then kissed her tears away.

He rolled to his side and tucked her against him, one arm around her waist.

She wiped the last of her tears, glad she wasn't facing him with all her stupid tears. "I need to get out of here. I have to go to class."

"You have a little time."

She felt raw, every nerve inside-out and exposed. Every cell in her body urged her to bolt.

He brushed her hair back and kissed her temple. "Just let me hold you a little longer."

"Hold me tight."

He did. She felt herself relaxing, her mind clearing,

her heart resuming a steady beat.

She'd nearly dozed off when he spoke again.

"Listen, I'm heading out to LA tonight."

She turned in his arms and stared at him, wide-awake now. "What?"

"Ty offered to help me find work. I haven't had any interest in my résumé at the airlines. They're not hiring right now."

"You just got here and now you're leaving?" It felt like a betrayal. First he got her nice and vulnerable with all his tenderness; then he pulled the rug out from under her.

"I need to work. I need to be worthy of you."

"You already are!"

"No, I'm not, but I want to try."

She jerked away. He grabbed her and she twisted out of his hold. "I can't believe you," she said, hating how her voice sounded all choked.

She got out of bed and dressed in quick jerky movements.

"Mad, come on. Give me a chance to make something of myself."

"I don't know where you get your screwed-up ideas about who deserves what or whatever—"

"You're not making any sense. I want the best for you."

She shoved her feet in her boots and grabbed her

messenger bag. "Enjoy LA."

"Would you wait? You're my ride."

She ground her teeth. "Fine."

She pulled out her cell phone to text Hailey about her shitty life, pointedly ignoring his naked body slowly covering up. Either way, naked or covered, he was irresistibly sexy and it annoyed her that she was still drawn to him when he was pissing her off so badly, abandoning her in her time of need.

She had a text from her dad. *Family meeting tonight re: mom.*

Great! Perfect! The fucking cherry on top!

That woman did *not* deserve the title of mom. Josh had told her the story of how their mom left the day after Christmas so she wouldn't ruin their holiday. Mad didn't remember any of it. She'd only just turned one. Josh and Jake had been eight, so they probably took it the worst. Ty, Alex, and Logan were six, five, and four respectively. She couldn't help but think that her being born three years after the last kid had been the last straw.

She paced back and forth, waiting for Park, who'd slipped into the bathroom. She stilled. You know what? Fine. She'd be at this stupid family meeting only because it was her house and she refused to hide out forever. It gave the woman too much power over her. She sent off a bunch of texts to her brothers, who replied predictably with variations of WTF. See? It wasn't just her that thought the woman was evil and her dad was an idiot to let her back in his life.

She drove back home, quietly seething about her life and everything happening in it out of her control.

"I'm coming back," Park said from the passenger seat. "It's just for a few days so I can meet Ty's people and see if it's a good fit. He got me a first-class ticket."

"How long have you known?"

"He gave it to me on New Year's Day just before he left. I know my timing sucks, but I wasn't sure if I was going to take him up on it until now. I need to do this for us."

"This is not for us, it's for you."

"I need a good job for our future," he insisted. "To give you everything you deserve."

She clamped her mouth shut. She knew he thought he was doing the right thing. Long experience told her that when Park got an idea in his head there was just no changing it. Too bad it sucked balls. Just like her life.

He squeezed her shoulder. "Come on, I can feel the tension radiating off you after I spent hours screwing it out of you."

She glared at him. He gave her a small tender smile she found hard to resist.

She sighed. "Dad called a family meeting tonight

about Tina." Even the name Tina left a bad taste in her mouth. "What the hell is wrong with Dad? I want to crack their skulls together to knock some sense into them. I mean, what's the point of them getting together at this stage in his life?"

"He's only fifty-three," Park pointed out. Cops could retire earlier than most careers with a full pension, so she supposed he wasn't exactly old.

She loosened her death grip on the steering wheel. "Damn it all. All that screwing we did is wasted because now I want to throttle her again."

"I wouldn't say wasted," he teased. "Filthy fun more like."

A reluctant smile tugged at her lips.

"Can I give you some advice?" he asked.

"No."

"She'll always be a part of you, but you don't have to let her rule you."

She scowled. "Where'd you get that from, a fortune cookie?"

"She doesn't have to be everything."

She blinked rapidly, not wanting to cry over that woman, who didn't deserve her tears.

He reached over and put a hand on her upper thigh. "Your dad told me that once about my mom."

"Oh good, I'll throw it in his face."

"Don't. I only said it to help you."

Nothing can help me.

She kept the bleak thought to herself, where it burned a hole in her gut.

~ ~ ~

"Mad, glad to see you here for the family meeting," her dad said, standing in front of the sofa where she sat.

She put her feet up on the coffee table and jerked her chin. "I live here."

"Tina will be down in a minute," her dad said.

"Fabulous."

Her dad rocked back and forth on his heels. A long silence fell. She refused to make it easier on him. He'd brought that woman into her house. The house where she'd grown up motherless. That evil, abandoning, unfeeling bitch. She struggled to find her calm center again.

So fucking perfect that Park was on his way to Ty on the other side of the country, trying to be what he thought she wanted. But did he ask her? No! Did she want him doing stunts? Hell no.

She jumped up and paced.

The front door opened. Josh and Logan stepped inside. She immediately felt better. Josh was a rock. Logan, she suddenly realized, took after their mom. His hair was a light brown, unlike the rest of them with dark brown hair. He had her narrow nose, same ski-jump tilt at the end. Still, he was one of them. They'd shared a room growing up, her on top bunk, him on bottom, and he'd been her long-time late night confidant. When he wasn't teasing her.

"I'm only here for you, Dad," Josh said, taking off his black wool coat and hanging it in the front closet. "I have nothing to say to the woman who abandoned her six children."

Mad went over and hugged Josh, so glad she wasn't alone in this. He kissed the top of her head and ruffled her hair. She didn't even complain about the hair thing.

Logan looked a little shell-shocked, not even taking off his black down jacket, just standing there staring at nothing. "I barely remember her."

"I do," Josh said. "Beauty queen, nose in the air, thinks she's better than the commoners she's forced to live with."

"I want you to hear her out," her dad said. "Alex coming?"

Josh spoke in a flat tone. "He doesn't want Viv to meet her grandmother. Felt it would be confusing to her if she's not going to stick around. Is she sticking around?"

"I hope so," her dad said.

Josh shot Mad a look that she understood

perfectly. *You believe this?*

Lucky for Jake he was missing all the drama, off on his honeymoon. Ty out in California would miss it too. She doubted Tina would stick around long enough to see them.

Tina walked downstairs, all grace and poise. "Hello."

"Hi," Logan said, watching her curiously.

Josh and Mad were silent.

"This is everyone," her dad said.

Tina nodded. "I understand." She stopped in the living room, where all of them were standing. Her blond hair was perfectly styled in waves to her shoulders. She wore a silk white blouse with a black pencil skirt and black heels. Completely overdressed and overly made up for a family meeting. But what could you expect? She'd probably never been to a family meeting. "So I want to start with saying how very sorry I am. I stayed away, ashamed to face all of you. I don't deserve forgiveness. I reconnected with your dad and he encouraged me to talk to you."

Mad, Josh, and Logan stared at her, silent. There was nothing to say. She was right. She didn't deserve forgiveness.

Tina turned to Josh first. "Hello, Josh. It's nice to see you again."

Josh said nothing.

"I understand Jake is skiing in the Swiss Alps," Tina said. "I've been. It's lovely."

Josh remained impassive, his expression giving nothing away.

Tina turned to Logan. "You're so tall. The spitting image of your grandfather at this age."

"Do you know how old I am?" Logan asked, no real rancor in his voice. Only curiosity. He studied her face like he was trying to memorize it or maybe remember it.

"Of course," Tina said smoothly. "You're twenty-nine. A mother never forgets the day she gave birth."

"You sure forgot a helluva lot in between," Josh said.

"Yeah," Mad said, piling on. "I didn't see any birthday cards coming in the mail."

"Or phone calls," Josh said.

"Or visits," Mad finished.

"I'm sorry," Tina said. "I had severe postpartum depression after I had Madison. I longed for escape. And when I got word that a former acquaintance was single, I jumped at the chance for the wealthy lifestyle he offered. I'm not proud of myself. I understand if you never want to forgive me."

They were all quiet.

"Why are you here now?" Josh asked.

She folded her hands in front of her. "I realized I

still love your dad. And my children, that love never goes away, though I don't expect you to feel the same way."

"And where is this wealthy acquaintance of yours?" Josh asked, his lip curling. "Dump you for a younger model?"

Tina flushed red and smoothed her hair back. "Things just didn't work out with him."

"I bet," Mad put in.

"That's enough," her dad snapped. "Tina has given you a humble apology and I expect you to speak to her respectfully."

"I'm out," Josh said. He grabbed his coat and left, the door shutting quietly behind him. It might as well have been a slam for the sudden tense silence.

Her dad let out a long breath. "Why don't you two have a seat," he said to Mad and Logan, the two youngest in the family.

Logan sat on the sofa, so Mad did too.

Her dad slid an arm around Tina. "Things have been going really well and we plan on getting remarried."

"After two weekends of middle-aged fucking?" Mad blurted.

Tina gasped. Her dad let the remark slide.

Logan shot her a look and then turned back to their dad. "What's the rush?"

"Tina needs a place to stay and we have plenty of room," her dad said.

"So shack up with her," Mad said. "I'm sure she'll bail again as soon as the next wealthy acquaintance puts out word he needs a trophy wife."

"I'm too old to be a trophy wife," Tina said, acting all modest.

"Get some plastic surgery," Mad suggested. "I'm sure you'll be snatched up by some old moneybags real quick."

"Mad," her dad said in a low warning.

Logan muttered under his breath at her, "No filter," and then louder, "Okay. Thanks for letting us know." He stood and snagged Mad's arm, pulling her with him. "We're going to go. Bye, Tina."

Mad went out the door with Logan, glad to get away from Tina. And especially the hold she seemed to have over Mad's dad.

Logan stopped on the sidewalk, quickly shed his black down jacket and settled it over her shoulders. She was too distraught to protest the big-brother move.

"You got somewhere to go for a couple weeks?" he asked.

"You think I should move out?"

"Yeah. I think if we leave them alone, she'll get bored and restless in the burbs and look for the next guy to latch onto."

"Ya think?"

He nodded. "You see how dolled up she was just for a Monday night family meeting? And there's dad in a flannel shirt and ancient jeans. He can't keep up with her. Couldn't back then and definitely not now."

"I so want to believe you're right."

"I'd invite you to my place, but Ethan's buddy's got the sofa."

"Nah, that's okay. I'll crash at Hailey's place. She owes me for snagging a robber at Ludbury House."

"Please tell me you're not doing citizen arrests."

"I'm not doing citizen arrests."

"Don't tell me anything else."

"I'm with Park now."

He flashed a smile. "Good for you. You've always loved him."

"How do you know that?"

He widened his eyes and made an adoring cow face. "Everyone knew how you worshipped him." Wow. Guess it wouldn't be as hard as she thought for her family to see her and Park as a couple.

"Now he worships me," she informed him.

"Where is he, anyway?"

"Out in LA with Ty."

Logan winced. "Did not see that coming. I can't believe Park would trash cars and bikes for stunts. He loves machines too much for that."

"Maybe he'll just jump out a window." She cringed thinking of that. Not her Park. She'd finally gotten him back out of war zones. "Augh! I can't think about it. See ya!"

He snagged the sleeve of his jacket, and she shrugged it off. "Keep me posted on Dad," he said.

"Yup."

She stepped back inside the house.

Her dad smiled at her, his arms wrapped around Tina. "We're going to Vegas!"

"Great, you saved me from moving out. Go nuts."

She went to the kitchen and got herself a drink. Talk about a midlife crisis. She wouldn't even try to talk sense into her dad. Let him crash and burn. Maybe then it would finally get through his brain that Tina was no good for him.

CHAPTER EIGHTEEN

Mad sat in the circle of eight women—her usual friends plus their newest members Missy, Sabrina, and Lexi—at the Happy Endings Book Club meeting at Something's Brewing Café, feeling anything but happy. She pretended to be listening to Hailey reading chapter one of *The Princess Bride* out loud. It was Thursday night, she'd had only the briefest of phone calls from Park out in LA, and her damn midlife-crisis dad hadn't returned yet from Vegas. She wasn't sure if he'd married Tina or not, but she was not looking forward to family functions with *that woman* in attendance. At least Hailey was back to her usual cheerful self, no longer worried about break-ins at work. The man had turned out to be homeless, displaced from a mental institution that didn't have the budget to keep him. He was now in a psychiatric hospital, getting the help he needed.

Someone snapped their fingers in her face and she

swatted them away.

"You okay?"

She jerked her head up to see Charlotte looking at her with some concern.

She straightened. "Yeah. Just tired." She suddenly noticed the women had gone quiet. She looked around at all the concerned faces, sensed it might be girl-talk time and just wasn't ready to go there. She didn't know some of the newcomers that well and every time she talked about Tina she wanted to kick someone's ass.

"I brought brownies!" Hailey chirped, lifting the lid off a large square plastic container. "So the game is tell us if you like your man inked and muscled or trim and in a business suit, and then you get a brownie."

"Can't we have both?" Charlotte asked.

"No, silly," Hailey said. "No man is both of those things."

Josh immediately came to mind, but Mad was too depressed to even try to tease Hailey. Besides, he didn't wear a business suit anymore.

Charlotte gestured for the brownies. "If I have to choose, I go with inked and muscled." She took the tiniest piece of a brownie.

"Good to know," Hailey said with a big wink.

Lauren took the container, said, "Business suit," and quickly popped a brownie in her mouth.

Everyone else picked inked and muscled, big surprise. Mad took the container and reached for a brownie, but Hailey snatched the container out of her hand.

"Nope," Hailey said. "You have to tell us which you prefer."

The women started joking around, eating their brownies, the same brownie being denied Mad, their conversation rising in volume with her temper.

Hailey waved the container around enticingly.

"Who cares?" Mad barked. Hailey knew she was stuck on Park. The big jerk.

"It's part of the game. Which kind of man do you prefer?" Hailey pressed.

Mad lost it. "You know what kind of man I prefer? The kind who sticks around!" She leapt to her feet in her agitation. "The kind who doesn't have some twisted sense of honor that makes him bail! The kind that's there for you when your biological mother decides to make an appearance for the first time in twenty-five years!"

The women were all staring at her, eyes wide, but there was no stopping her now.

She punched a fist in the air. "The kind who is man enough to stand by your side after making love to you so tenderly that he makes you cry!"

"Uh, Mad," Lauren started.

"No!" Mad said, shaking her head for emphasis. "I won't be nice!"

"Um…" Hailey said, her head tilting to the side.

Mad jabbed a finger at Hailey. "You want sharing?" she barked. "Parker Shaw still thinks he knows what's best for me. Did he ask me if I want him to get a job throwing himself out windows and leaping off motorcycles? No! Does he care that my dad is marrying my mom and it makes me want to puke? No!" She yanked the V in her ripped shirt down to show them her hawk tattoo. "Does he care that this tattoo is a constant reminder that he's got a hold of my heart?"

"I care," a deep voice said.

"Aaaaahhh!" She let out a high-pitched girly scream, her entire body jerking with ungraceful shock. She whirled, face flaming. "Park."

"I didn't realize you shared so much at book club," he said drily.

The women tittered.

She crossed to him, about to give him hell for sneaking up on her like that when he grabbed her in a bear hug and nuzzled into her neck.

"I missed you," he whispered.

The fury left her in a whoosh. "I missed you too."

"I can't do stunts with Ty. They're destroying too many good motorcycles. I can't bear the carnage."

Her knees went weak with relief.

He brushed her hair back and cupped her jaw, his gaze warm and tender. "I'm home for good. I've got savings and I can open my own shop, fixing cars or bikes. Maybe both. I'll figure it out." He stroked her cheek. "I'm sorry I wasn't the man who stuck around like you needed. I will from now on." He kissed her and spoke against her lips. "Forever."

Her cheeks heated at the sudden mushy intensity because she knew he meant it. He was a man of honor, a man of his word. She threw her arms around him and kissed him passionately. Her friends hooted and hollered. She broke the kiss and turned to them. "Anyone have leads on clients for Park, let me know. He can fix anything with an engine."

"I love working on planes," Park said, "but I can do cars and bikes too."

"My brother-in-law just lost his best mechanic," Missy said. "The guy moved to Florida. Do you like classic cars?" Classic cars meant big money.

Park smiled widely. "Do I like classic cars?" He whooped. "Does a grease monkey like grease? Yes! I'd love to." He strode quickly over to Missy for the contact info. Hailey handed him Mad's coat and messenger bag. Then he stood in the circle of women, beautiful one and all, but his eyes were only for her. "You all mind if I steal this beauty? I've missed her something fierce."

"Aww," the women chorused.

"Go!" Hailey said. "Shoo. We don't need her kind here. This club is for single ladies." She gave Mad a wink and a smile.

Park slipped an arm around her shoulders and guided her out the door. "The job is at Exotic and Classic Car Restorations. Nico Marino runs it. That place is awesome."

"I had no idea they needed someone there." Hailey's magic at work. She'd connected Missy into the self-defense class and then book club and that connected to her and Park.

He stopped on the sidewalk in front of the café and helped her on with her coat. "Did your dad get remarried?"

"I have no idea." She zipped up the coat. "He's been out of touch and it's been three days."

Park stiffened. "You want to send Ty out there to check on him? He's closest."

She took her messenger bag from him and tucked it over her shoulder. "Give it a little more time. I'm sure he's fine. Probably just living it up."

"Or nursing his broken heart because she left him again."

Her jaw dropped. She hadn't thought of that.

"Just saying."

"Yeah, call Ty."

"I will, but first…" He went down on one knee.

"Aah!" she shrieked in the second girly scream of her life. A cheer went up nearby and she turned to see her friends on the other side of the large picture window, watching, bright eyed and eager. She turned back to Park. "Yes."

He smiled, his hazel eyes warm and tender. "Let me ask you the question first."

"I worship you."

He chuckled. "I worship you too. Will you be my wife so I can do that for the rest of my life?"

"Yes!"

He reached into his pocket, pulled out a round diamond ring and slid it on her finger.

She stared at it. "Where did you get this?"

"LA." He rose in one fluid motion and held her ring hand between his two large hands. He smiled into her eyes. "Do you like it?"

"Yes!" the women hollered through the window.

She looked at her friends, grinned, and turned back to Park. "It's unanimous. Yes."

And then her friends rushed out the front door to hug and congratulate them both. It was a little nuts with all their jumping-up-and-down enthusiasm. Hailey was so thrilled they got to witness the proposal she promptly made Park an honorary book club member. There was really no polite way to say no.

EPILOGUE

"Boxers, briefs, or boxer briefs?" Hailey asked. Once again she was digging for the nitty-gritty at the Happy Endings Book Club meeting.

The women leaned in. Except Mad, who rolled her eyes and crossed her black work boots over each other.

"Boxer briefs," Park answered honestly.

Hailey scribbled that down in a notebook.

Park was the token male, honorary book club member, and her devoted fiancé. It was Mad's spring break and she'd finally, after much prodding on Hailey's part, dragged Park along to book club. He'd been pretty cool about the whole thing. Probably because he was in good spirits because, after four months of intense training under his new boss, Nico Marino, Park had his first solo project, a 1988 Ferrari F40. Or maybe he was just used to a mouthy woman in his face, though Park always made Mad sound better than that. He called her sassy. A bunch of other cute girly names too. Was it any wonder she loved him?

Hailey looked up from her notebook, her brows drawn together in concentration. "Now what do guys think about after a first date?"

Park shot Mad a sly look. "They think where's this hot babe been all my life? Is this the same twerpy kid that told all the guys to grow a pair?"

"Be serious, please," Hailey said. "We've all had a number of underwhelming post-date experiences. Men who don't call—"

"Who vague-text you three days later," Charlotte added.

"Who don't show up on your second date and you just keep waiting and waiting, hoping he was in a car accident," Lauren said sweetly.

Park cleared his throat. "I'm really not sure how my answer will help with the general male population. Don't you want a larger sample size?"

"Can you get us one?" Hailey asked. "They have to be single."

"You bet." He turned to Mad. "Whadda ya think? Bring your brothers in on this?" He meant her single brothers and blood brothers, the honorary brothers they'd grown up with.

Mad nodded. "Ty will be back for a job in the city in a couple weeks. You definitely want to hear from him. He'll tell it like it is."

Park inclined his head. "Four single Campbells, four blood brothers, plus me should give you a good start. Is this for some kind of research paper?"

The women laughed uproariously.

Park shot Mad a questioning look. She lifted one shoulder. How to explain that romantic Hailey, book club leader and wedding planner, thought she could make happy endings happen? Of course, that required luring more single men in close enough to snag. Mad wouldn't be the one to stand in her way. The woman had stood by her side, a constant cheerleader, while Mad painfully took her heart out of cold storage and put it on the line for Park. Now here they were engaged. They'd be married in a little over a year, the month after she graduated with her college degree. Park said he wanted her to come into the marriage with a degree. In the meantime, they shacked up in a cheap one-bedroom apartment in Eastman, happily fornicating like beasts.

Hailey clapped. "Yay!" She frowned. "Wait, how will you get them here?"

"Easy," Park said. "We move this over to Garner's. Offer them free food and a brewski."

Hailey's pale blue eyes widened. "Now why didn't I think of that?"

"You're not a guy," Park said.

Hailey smiled, a bemused expression on her face. "And Josh will be trapped behind the bar."

"Muah-ha-ha," Mad said, "you evil genius."

"Maybe we should invite your dad too," Hailey said to Mad. "Now that he's single. It seems like he might want to meet someone new."

Her dad had returned from Vegas without Tina. Not because Tina bailed. Because her dad realized, despite the love he still had for Tina, he couldn't forgive her for her late return in their children's lives. Her dad had hoped the family meeting would help heal the scars he believed his kids carried from not having their mom around, but, as they later explained to him, none of them had ever felt lacking in love thanks to his big heart. For Mad, seeing Tina again was too little, too late and she didn't want a relationship with her mom at this point in her life. Her brothers felt the same way. Some good had come out of it, though, her dad said his brief nostalgic time with Tina had made him realize he was ready for a new relationship.

"Bring him," Park said. "He's cool. And he's seen it all, believe me."

"But no matchmaking for him," Mad warned Hailey. "He's my dad." She shuddered. She was happy for him to meet someone—he'd been alone for so many years—she just didn't want to witness it happening.

"We shall see," Hailey replied and then with a mischievous smile she turned to Park. "Vibrating purple butterfly thong or boy shorts?"

Park licked his lips and looked to Mad, who shot out of her seat. She'd recently bought exactly that and Hailey knew it.

Park stood. "You have something you want to tell me?"

She grabbed his hand and tugged him toward the door. They'd interrogated her man long enough. He followed eagerly behind her.

"Ooh, baby!" Charlotte called.

"Me-ow!" Ally said.

There was a bunch of hooting and catcalling, but it all faded in the distance as Park's arms wrapped around her from behind. "Sugar, you're going down," he whispered.

She turned to look at him over her shoulder. "That's my line."

"Minx."

She grinned. He shifted, scooping her up into his arms and carrying her out the door. She heard a collective sigh as the door shut behind them.

"You're setting the bar high for my friends," Mad told him. "What with all your romantic gestures and all."

"Good, they should be treated well," he replied. "And if they're not, I'll kick the guy's ass."

"Me too."

"Deal."

~THE END~

Dear Readers,

The frenemies continue! What do you think Josh will do once he finds out Hailey's been squashing his dating prospects with his unfortunate condition? At least they gave each other one moment of peace on New Year's Eve. Charlotte and Ty got off to a rocky start, but now that Ty's coming back to town for a job he wants a second chance at making a good impression. Would you like an exclusive sneak peek at my next release? Just sign up for my newsletter at www.kyliegilmore.com/newsletter and you'll receive sneak peeks, excerpts, and subscriber-only giveaways. Next up is Ty and Charlotte's story, *So Revealing*, book 3 in the Happy Endings Book Club series. Join the club and get your happy ending!

So Revealing (Happy Endings Book Club #3)
The last thing Charlotte Vega needs is a cocky HOT stuntman like Ty Campbell in her life. But when he pulls the ultimate stunt—a sexy romantic gesture that ends with a charming invitation to a sunset dinner cruise—she finds him impossible to resist. Cue disaster.

   Their rocky first date goes from bad to worse when

his yacht (okay, it's actually borrowed and he's only had one boating lesson) gets stranded in deep mud. Turns out there's nothing Ty can do but wait hours and hours for high tide with no power, no way to cook dinner, and a hangry sexy-as-hell woman.

But Ty is determined to salvage the date so he starts a game to pass the time. Only what Ty learns makes him realize he may have just botched a date with the perfect woman. How will he ever win her now?

Sign up for my newsletter to be notified when the third book, *So Revealing*, releases at www.kyliegilmore. com.

Also by Kylie Gilmore

The Clover Park Series

THE OPPOSITE OF WILD (Book 1)

DAISY DOES IT ALL (Book 2)

BAD TASTE IN MEN (Book 3)

KISSING SANTA (Book 4)

RESTLESS HARMONY (Book 5)

NOT MY ROMEO (Book 6)

REV ME UP (Book 7)

AN AMBITIOUS ENGAGEMENT (Book 8)

CLUTCH PLAYER (Book 9)

A TEMPTING FRIENDSHIP (Book 10)

The Clover Park STUDS Series

ALMOST IN LOVE (Book 1)

ALMOST MARRIED (Book 2)

ALMOST OVER IT (Book 3)

ALMOST ROMANCE (Book 4)

ALMOST HITCHED (Book 5)

Happy Endings Book Club Series

HIDDEN HOLLYWOOD (Book 1)

INVITING TROUBLE (Book 2)

Acknowledgments

Big jumping hugs to my readers! I couldn't do any of this without you! Special thanks to my brother-in-law, who inspired my honorable Air Force hero. Thank you for your service to our country. Mucho thanks also to my family, Tessa, Pauline, Paul, Mimi, Kim, and Jenn for all you do.

About the Author

Kylie Gilmore is the *USA Today* bestselling author of the Happy Endings Book Club series, the Clover Park series, and the Clover Park STUDS series. She writes quirky, tender romance with a solid dose of humor.

Kylie lives in New York with her family, two cats, and a nutso dog. When she's not writing, wrangling kids, or dutifully taking notes at writing conferences, you can find her flexing her muscles all the way to the high cabinet for her secret chocolate stash.

Praise for Kylie Gilmore

THE OPPOSITE OF WILD

"This book is everything a reader hopes for. Funny. Hot. Sweet."
—New York Times Bestselling Author, Mimi Jean Pamfiloff

"It's intriguing and complex while still being light hearted and truly romantic. To see a male so twisted and turned is unusual but honestly made the book all the more enjoyable."
—Harlequin Junkie

"Ms. Gilmore's writing style draws the reader in and does not let go until the very end of the story and leaves you wanting more."
—Romance Bookworm

"Every aspect of this novel touched me and left me unable to put it down. I pulled an all-nighter, staying up until after 3 am to get to the last page."
—Luv Books Galore

DAISY DOES IT ALL

"The characters in this book are downright hilarious sometimes. I mean, when you start a book off with a fake life and immediately follow it by a rejected proposal, you know that you are in for a fun ride."
—The Little Black Book Blog

"Daisy Does It All is a sweet book with a hint of sizzle. The characters are all very real and I found myself laughing along with them and also having my heart ripped in two for them."
—A is for Alpha, B is for Book

BAD TASTE IN MEN

"I gotta dig a friends to lovers story, and Ms. Gilmore's 3rd book in the Clover Park Series hits the spot. A great dash of humor, a few pinches of steam, and a whole lotta love…Gilmore has won me over with everything I've read and she's on my auto buy list…she's on my top list of new authors for 2014."
—Storm Goddess Book Reviews

"The chemistry between the two characters is so real and so intense, it will have you turning the pages into the midnight hour. Throw in a bit of comedy – a dancing cow, a sprained ankle, and a bit of jealousy and Gilmore has a recipe for great success."
—Underneath the Covers blog

KISSING SANTA

"I love that Samantha and Rico are set up by none other than their mothers. And the journey they go on is really hilarious!! I laughed out loud so many times, my kids asked me what was wrong with me."
—Amazeballs Book Addicts

"I absolutely adored this read. It was quick, funny, sexy and got me in the Christmas spirit. Samantha and Rico are a great couple that keep one another all riled up in more ways than one, and their sexual tension is super hot."
—Read, Tweet, Repeat

RESTLESS HARMONY

"Kylie's writing as usual is full of laugh out loud humor, touching moments, and heat that will make you fan yourself… If you are looking for a book that will having you laughing out loud and feeling good when you are done, this book is for you."
—Smut and Bonbons blog

"My heart broke for Gabe's past, but it soared for the understanding and love in which he got through from a family born of true love and commitment. Kylie brought the real with this one. Heartache, love, support, sexiness, and beliefs."
—Reading by the Book blog

NOT MY ROMEO

"Their sexual tension and continuous banter had me smiling. I couldn't get enough and stayed up late just to finish their story, because I had to know where it went."
—Book Junky Girls blog

"They may not have been Romeo and Juliet, but they sure made one hell of a story that kept me laughing and reading on."
—Smut and Bonbons blog

REV ME UP

"The way Lily and Nico met cracked me up. Let's just say it was a wild case of mistaken identity! It pulled me in and I couldn't put the book down!"
—Romance Novel Giveaways blog

"It was a mission to make the sexy 'wrong' redhead see how wonderful and lovable she really was. It was giving her the family she desired and longed for. It was Clover Park series perfection. Love. Italian wedding cookies. Unity. Forever."
—Reading by the Book blog

"Rev Me Up is a heartwarming fun read. Kylie infuses her sense of humor in the heroine that I always enjoy reading and the men in Clover Park make me want to pay it a visit!"
—Smut and Bonbons blog

ALMOST IN LOVE

"Ms. Gilmore is an excellent storyteller, and her main characters are hard to forget, but her secondary characters are equally impressive. This is a character-driven tale inside of a sweet plot to get two nice people to fall in love and have their HEA."
—*USA Today*, Happy Ever After blog

"Forget alpha-male billionaires. The Studs will have you panting for that guy in nerdy glasses."
—New York Times Bestselling Author,
Mimi Jean Pamfiloff

"I was pulled in quickly and between the fascinating characters, the witty banter, the flow of the story and the emotions I was feeling I was blown away! I loved every second."
—A Beautiful Book blog

Thanks!

Thanks for reading *Inviting Trouble*. I hope you enjoyed it. Would you like to know about new releases? You can sign up for my new release email list at kyliegilmore.com/newsletter. I promise not to clog your inbox! Only new release info and some fun giveaways. You can also sign up by scanning this QR code:

I love to hear from readers! You can find me at:
kyliegilmore.com
Facebook.com/KylieGilmoreToo
Twitter @KylieGilmoreToo

If you liked Park and Mad's story, please leave a review on your favorite retailer's website or Goodreads. Thank you!

Made in the USA
Middletown, DE
23 March 2017